D1480864

Date Due

STAKING CLAIMS

Staking Claims

stories by
Page Edwards

Marion
Boyars

LONDON
BOSTON

First published simultaneously in Great Britain and the
United States in 1980 by Marion Boyars Publishers Ltd.
18 Brewer Street, London W1R 4AS and
Marion Boyars Publishers Inc.
99 Main St, Salem, New Hampshire 03079
Australian distribution by Thomas C. Lothian
4-12 Tattersalls Lane, Melbourne, Victoria 3000.

© Page Edwards, 1980
British Library Cataloguing in Publication Data
Edwards, Page
Staking Claims.
I. Title
823' .9' IFS   PS3555. D95S
ISBN 0 7145 2689 4 cloth edition
Library of Congress Catalog Card Number 79-66572

Printed and Bound in Canada
By The Hunter Rose Company Ltd.

CONTENTS

for
Amy
and
Ben
with
love

Lovely
Anne
Ketchum

AT ONE TIME, Don Ketchum owned almost half the upper valley above the village of Sharps Crossing and was a prosperous, hard working dairy farmer. When his interest in milk left him, he divided the land, parcel by parcel, into smaller farms and summer places, and he was left with a twenty acre field, a run-down farm house, an auto repair shop and a woodlot. Rusted machinery, sugaring equipment and a cider press cluttered his leaning barn which sheltered three snowmobiles, each a year older than the next. To help out, his wife wound bobbins for the textile factory in Bellows Falls.

At home, she unpacked the skeins of yarn and fitted them onto the spindle and worked the ancient winder and, sometimes, she dreamed. Anne's wish was to provide the women of Sharps Crossing with a clean, friendly place where they could come each week for a wash and set and a confidential chat. For sure, Alice Cowper did the women's hair now. They made their appointments and went to her house. But Anne did not feel comfortable in Alice's living-room arched over a plastic sink on wheels with a trash barrel under the drain. She wanted, and assumed the other women did as well, an authentic hair parlor.

Oh, Alice could relax a person, that was certain. When she tapped the dryer and mouthed 'you're done' over the rush of air and the motor's noise, Anne always came out from under feeling strangely empty. 'Good Lord,' she said, 'What was I talking about? It seems I come here, Alice, and can't keep my mouth shut.'

Alice took the three dollars she pressed confidentially into her palm, though no one was in the room, and said, 'It's fast with me.' She tapped her scarf which obscured a confusion of pins and rollers. 'Whatever you say, Anne, it's fast in here with me.'

Her curls tight, her scalp alive from the attention, she left Alice Cowper's always feeling, vaguely, that she had exposed too much of herself. The mood which Alice imposed on the appointment made her, Anne knew, open herself too wide. But, as the bluish suds rose above her head, as the long fingers worked on her scalp, as the stream of piercing hot water melted what little reserve she had–week after week–without thinking about it, Anne emptied herself to Alice, who listened to her . . .

Evenings, when her husband went back to the shop, Anne, in pursuit of her dream, began to practice on her own hair, styling herself over the kitchen sink. One night she would climb into bed coiffured for a ball, her black hair piled high on her head with two small, tight curls at each temple. Another, she would go to sleep as a young girl who might well be off for a picnic with her lover, hair curled slightly at the ends, wisps falling onto her shoulders. Or she would turn herself into a sturdy peasant flying across a field on horseback, hair parted in the middle, pulled loosely over the ears and caught in a single, thick plait in back. How lovely she looked then with her face framed, her smooth olive colored face.

When her husband returned home late and did not bother to wash thoroughly, the gasoline odor he brought up to their bed and the faint smell of beer dissolved what perfume there was in her dreams. Her costume ball became a church supper; her picnic, a jeep ride with a chain saw; the bracing horseback ride, a fast and loud career on his snowmobile over the hay fields which he had once owned. When he kissed her on those nights, she responded to his smothering lips, and he mistook her desperate attempts to recapture her faulted dreams for desire.

One morning, a young man, who was dressed like a western wrangler, appeared at Ketchum's shop. His pick-up truck had a leaking radiator and there was a short in the electrical system. He wore a light green hat whose brim had been trimmed ragged and a sparse redish beard which made him look more elf than wrangler, but he could sure handle the tools. When Rainbow asked for a job, Ketchum hired the strange elfish youth on the spot. The first week, he lived in the back of his truck. During one period of solid rain, rain so relentless Rainbow's truck sank to its lug nuts in the mud, Ketchum suggested to his wife that the young man might rent the small room, the cold room, off the kitchen and take his meals with them. After all, they didn't use the cold room and had no plans for it.

'It's fine with me, if he takes off his hat to eat,' she said.

Anne found Rainbow a cast iron bed frame in the barn and a

wobbly cardboard dresser and a cane chair with the seat poked through. He used some barn boards for shelves, hung his posters and rewired an electric fireplace. She gave him a corner of the refrigerator for his beef jerky, organic peanut butter, sesame seeds, dates.

Evenings, while Ketchum finished up a job at the shop, he sat in the cold room in front of the simulated fire in the electric fireplace and played his guitar. Anne liked the music drifting through the kitchen and practised on her hair while she listened. One night something happened which she would never forget. Wearing only her dungarees and a brassier, she was bent over the kitchen sink. He came out of the cold room to get a magazine or a glass of milk–she never was certain what he wanted. She spun towards him, covering her front with a towel. Her huge dark eyes held at once a startled hurt look. She was angry with surprise, but pleased, strangely, and her eyes showed it. Without speaking, he turned and went back into the cold room. That Rainbow had seen her almost undressed always caused a warm wave of pleasure to sweep over her. After Rainbow had gone away, when she and her husband sat silently in the living room, she could evoke that pleasure and hold it within her for hours. From then on, Anne practiced on her hair in the afternoons and she asked Rainbow to sit in the living room with her and play after her husband had returned to the shop.

The evenings they spent together would sustain her in her loneliness. He played his guitar while she sat, legs crossed, on the couch sewing something of her own or mending his or her husband's working clothes. She enjoyed his slow, even voice. It was gentle enough so that she could give in to it and become surrounded by mystery and wonderment. At those times, she lost herself and had feelings that she had not allowed herself since she was a young girl in Chippenhook. As she listened (she could not look at him while he sang) she was carried to the Rockies and to Wyoming, far to the west where she had never been, carried on the thread of his song, and she slowly came to realize that if she and Rainbow were alone enough, one night they would make love.

They would make love, she supposed, the way her dog
Bonnie eagerly jumped into Rainbow's lap and put her paws on
either shoulder and, unconcerned about the guitar, licked his
face and beard. He put the instrument aside and encouraged
the little terrier until she was exhausted and had to go into the
kitchen and lie down. Anne sewed and supposed that making
love with Rainbow would be just as exhausting for her and that
afterwards she would have to go up to her own bed and that she
would be as pleasantly exhilarated after so many hours and
hours of love. She never had any misgivings about those
thoughts or about how peculiar their evenings alone together
seemed to the village women or how strange and improper
(even whorish, according to Alice Cowper) it was to have a
young man in the same house at night without her husband
present.

One afternoon, as the blue suds began to rise and the fingers
began to soothe Anne's scalp, Alice asked her, 'That boy still
up to your place, Mrs. Ketchum?'

'Oh yes, he's still with us, Alice.'

'That's some back he's got.'

'I'm sorry?'

'A hunk of man. Healthy. How old is he?'

'I'm afraid I can't tell you that. You know, I've never asked.
Goodness. We know each other so well and of all the things we
talk about, I've never thought to ask. I suppose I should. He's
not more than twenty, I shouldn't suppose.'

She could feel Alice lighten her touch. She sensed Alice's
curiousity. Vaguely, she knew what that dry and pointed
curiousity would do to her in the village, yet she went on
talking. "He is a really wonderful man. I think I could love him
like a son. Don says that he's marvelously good at the shop. I
mean, he's so alive, so terribly alive, Alice. You can't imagine.
The house hums when he's there like it never has before,
especially when Don's not home. You should hear him play the
guitar.'

He actually did fill the house. She wanted him to fill it.
Ducking out from under Alice's hands in order to look into her
face, Anne said, 'I really enjoy him there with us. I want him

there. He's just like his name for me. It may sound silly, but Rainbow is *my* rainbow. He makes me happy.'

Alice rubbed her hair with a towel, as she usually did before putting her under the dryer. 'He must be a temptation. At night. A real temptation.'

'Of course he is. You know, sometimes I think I am going to throw myself at him.'

'Just like that?'

'Certainly. I think about it especially while he's playing. It's impossible of course. It wouldn't be fair to anyone, not to Don or him or me, when you think about it.'

She paid Alice and went home where she sat in the empty kitchen. She always said too much to Alice. Always. Always. Always.

Well, Alice could say whatever she wanted to anyone. What Anne wanted to know was why she had talked too much. Especially about him to her. It could only drive him away from her. She leaned on the kitchen table covering her head and was thoroughly overtaken by a deep-seated ache of loneliness.

Not less than two nights later, her husband came to supper sullen.

Anne ate, silently waiting for what she knew was coming, and did not allow herself to respond when Ketchum said, 'Stew two nights running.'

'It's always better the second time,' Rainbow said. 'Are you going back down after? We could finish up Dupree's truck.'

'I'll do that myself.'

To her, Ketchum's voice sounded hollow. She knew that her husband was not angry, she knew that he knew perfectly well that he had absolutely no grounds for jealousy, but he didn't sound like himself, only hollow as if somebody else had put the words in him. That's what finally hurt her. That's what made her change so much that the village women would persist in calling her "that lovely Anne Ketchum" and treat her as if she were an object too delicate, removed from their ordinary lives. Anne waited, knowing he was going to say the words that he *had* to say, not the words he knew, and her body went numb seeing his entire lack of emotion.

' . . . stay right where you are,' she heard him say. 'That's what you want. I've got ears. Everybody in town knows what's going on in this house behind my back. Don't think I don't, Mister Rainbow, or whoever the hell you are. I don't mind you living here. I don't mind working with you. But let me tell you what I do mind . . . what I mind like hell . . . '

'What's that, Don?' Her voice was a sieve, buzzing and breathless. 'Just what is it that you do mind?'

The look he gave her then caused her eyes to dart around the room. She looked at the plate in front of her, at the empty chair across from Rainbow. Eyes soft now, and liquid, she looked at Rainbow. 'You'd best go,' she said, quietly, returning her gaze to her half-eaten supper. 'I'm terribly sorry.'

She sensed that her husband was about to speak and looked up to hear the words that didn't belong to him come out of his mouth. She winced as her husband stabbed Rainbow in the shoulder with his finger. 'The boy knows why. You both know.'

Rainbow left the table, and she heard his plate drop in the sink and the door to the cold room close.

'I've . . . I . . . I know what you've heard, Don, but people don't know what they're saying sometimes,' she said, not looking at him.

'I want him out of my house,' he said.

Erect now in her chair, she sat not looking at anything and waited until Rainbow had left the house . . .

Don and Anne Ketchum have never again mentioned the young boy called Rainbow who once lived in the cold room off the kitchen. These days, her husband stays home after supper and, most evenings, if she's not too tired, Anne practices on her hair. Afterwards, she dresses and sits in the small rocker by the stove, facing her husband while he does the books. They don't say very much to one another in the evenings. But, everyone in the village knows how proud he is of his wife, and everyone knows what real trouble that lovely Anne Ketchum puts herself through every night to look good for her husband. Everyone knows, you can be certain.

Ketchum is proud, and afraid. At least once each evening he will look across the room at her bare shoulders, pale in the reflection of the lamp, and at her skin, which is still olive and smooth, almost porcelain. And a shiver will pass through him, sometimes, at the figure of his small, quiet wife. She seems to him, sometimes, like a statue so beautiful and, at the same time, so fleshless and remote, that he almost hesitates to touch her. And her eyes, Anne's lovely dark eyes, seem to him to have become, somehow, empty. And, in the late evening, if her eyes do meet his, he looks immediately at the rug, thankful that she is still there. For these days Ketchum is waiting, he has become certain that one evening when he looks across the room at his wife she, in her solitude, will not raise her eyes to his for she will not know that he is there at all.

The
Hired
Hand

I FIRST SAW my wife just over a year ago. At the time, I was a traveling representative for a small motel supply company. My home office was in Manchester, New Hampshire, and my territory extended as far north as Burlington, Vermont, and east to Lubec in Maine. When I saw her, I was headed towards Sharps Crossing, Vermont, to sell supplies to a new fourteen unit prefab. For the past week, I had been working my way south of the Vermont side of the Connecticut River. Earlier that day, I had passed through Bradford and stopped at a seven unit motor court in Fairlee near the rare bird and animal farm. After lunch, I cut over the hills to the west for Tunbridge, where I sold a case of room deodorant. Then I followed the West Branch of the Ompompanoosuc south towards Sharps Crossing, driving with the windows down. It was a brilliant afternoon in early spring, and she stood nude on the river bank. For me, our courtship began the moment she dove into the roily, brown water below the bridge. Her white body was tossed by the turbulence as she was swept downstream stroking out strong with the current. Bobbing, twisting with the waves, she rode the flood a good distance downstream before tucking quickly and disappearing underwater. I hurried from the car and held onto the railing while I pried off my shoes. I was fully prepared to jump in after her. Then, a moment later, all white and shivering, she climbed out on the opposite bank far down stream. She made her way back to the bridge through the willows and I watched.

All along the riverbank the thaw had set in. Snowfields were receding on the south face of the gentle, rolling hills, and new buds on the young beech and maples gave the brown riverbank and surrounding landscape a light green hue, like a mist drifting above the swollen river as it meandered in the fertile bottomland.

When she had recovered the distance the river had taken her, she plunged in a second time. Bucking the current, she swam almost directly across the current for her towel and clothes. After she had dried herself and dressed, she climbed up the steep bank and stomped onto the wooden planked bridge towards me. Her hair was wrapped in a white towel.

'Hey!'

'Hey what?'

'You were watching me. Aren't you embarrassed?'

I pulled back from the bridge rail and yelled above the current which seemed to hiss under me. 'I thought you were trying to kill yourself,' I said. The swiftness and color of the water below was exhilarating.

'So you slam on your brakes to watch!' she said. 'I don't think I believe you.' She was completely self-possessed, the afternoon was hers alone.

I discovered that I was holding my shoes and offered them to her as evidence of my resolve to jump in after her. We both looked down at my socks. When she began to laugh, I joined her. She laughed with her head thrown back, laughed harder than I did. The graceful lines of her neck and the fullness of her body, which was now animated with laughter, made it difficult for me to laugh with equal abandon. Her towel released itself and fell over the railing.

'Your towel,' I said, sincerely hoping she wouldn't ask me to go in after it.

She dismissed the towel making a bird-like gesture with her hand. 'Would you jump in after a person?' she asked. 'I mean would you really?'

'You didn't need any help,' I said.

'I don't mean me. I mean anyone.'

'Sure. If somebody needed help, I'd jump in after him.' I looked away from her, hoping I didn't seem overly courageous or a fool. 'You surprised me,' I said. 'That's all.'

'Oh, I do that every year. It's nothing. You should put on your shoes.'

As we got into my car, a jeep truck approached and squeezed by us. She waved to the driver. Cool, removed, he nodded and flicked on the yellow revolving flasher on the truck's cab.

'A friend?' I asked.

'A neighbor and sometimes a friend. You can turn around in Alice Cowper's driveway. Watch for pot holes. You'll splash mud up the side of her house. We live just up there on the right. I'm Sarah. Sarah Burns.'

'Phillip Boone. No relation to Daniel. I sell motel supplies.'
'I thought it was something like that,' she said. 'Do you actually enjoy selling that stuff? I mean, it's so depressing.'
'It gets me around,' I said. 'No, I don't like it.'
She was quiet for the remainder of the ride. At home, before she got out of the car, she said, 'Are you sure that's what you are? You don't look like a salesman, not really.'
'Then, I'm not one. What am I?'
She made her eyes flash. 'You're a man who watches naked women instead of working. That's what. I hope you get fired.'
She got out of the car and slammed the door. Then, she turned and said through the window. 'Well, Phillip Boone, aren't you coming in?'

Sarah introduced me to her mother and went upstairs.

Rosemary Burns was preparing supper and spoke to me from the kitchen, while I balanced a cup of coffee on my lap. 'I was alarmed too, at first,' she said. 'Especially when she was younger. But no one, I mean no one, can keep her out of the river on a day like today. When the thaw sets in for certain, she's in the river. She's done it every year since she was nine or ten.'

My first thought on seeing Rosemary Burns was that Sarah would look just like her one day. I liked that thought. They are the same height, have the same oval face and dark eyes. The same build–large women but not plump, not masculine. We have a picture of Rosemary on the soap stone stove in the parlor that was taken when she was young and the similarity is remarkable. It is a photograph of Rosemary's high school graduation. She was by far the most womanly looking of all the graduates. Her hair, which was darker then and hung well below her shoulders, flowed in long relaxed curls over the black graduation gown. Her hip bones, prominent in the photograph, protruded and her large breasts parted the pleating in front. She is standing erect on the platform, smiling. Her eyes are directed at someone to the right of the camera. A beautiful, strong, large-boned girl, infinitely more worldly than her classmates. I asked her once who she is looking at with such kindness and love and she told me Ralph, whom she married less than an hour and a half after that photograph was taken. She was pregnant with her first daughter, which might account for the look in her eyes.

I'm certain my being alone with Rosemary that first afternoon had a lot to do with my falling in love with Sarah. It occurs to me now that I was witnessing Sarah at age fifty. I liked what I saw. Sometimes, I think that I fell for the farm or for Rosemary before I actually fell for Sarah, which, I admit, must seem a sort of backwards way of doing it.

'Once each spring,' Rosemary was saying, 'she goes down to the bridge by Ketchum's garage and jumps in. I did it myself many times. I used to.' She went into the kitchen and returned with a plate of cookies. Sarah, in her room above us, scraped chairs and banged bureau drawers. 'I suppose we, each of us, thaw out differently. I mean, at my age, I can't skinny dip in the river anymore.'

Rosemary had a flirtatious tendency and I saw it then for the first time. A sort of devilish spark comes alive in her eyes and she seems to be letting you in on a secret or making you an intimate promise.

Outside, a small, thin woman carrying a basket of greens walked across the front lawn. Rosemary stopped her girlish flirting and went to the front door. 'That's a nice bunch of greens there, Anne,' she said.

'Oh yes, aren't they. How much salt pork should I use?'

'Two chunks. Two good sized chunks.'

'About half a pound?'

'Chop it up real fine, Anne.'

Rosemary closed the door and wiped her hands on her apron, though they were neither soiled nor wet. 'That happens the same way every year. Anne Ketchum and I don't say too much the rest of the time. With Sarah it's the river. With Anne it's her greens. With Ralph it's breaking ground in the garden and bringing in the parsnips. I poach them for him in milk and butter.' She fingered her watch, stretching the band to see it better. 'Goodness, look at the time. You'll stay for supper, Phillip?'

A few minutes later, I heard Ralph in the kitchen. 'Here's

your parsnips,' he said.

'Watch the floor. I just washed it. Your boots are muddy.'

'Plenty of milk?' he asked.

'There's some from breakfast. Don't bother.'

'I'll be in after I milk them.'

'We'll all be ready for you.'

'What's that New Hampshire car in the driveway?'

'A friend of Sarah's. He'll be staying for supper.'

The screen door closed. It always took Ralph forty-five minutes to milk and bed down the cows. It takes me more like an hour. But, it used to take even longer than that.

Sarah came downstairs wearing a dress. Though her mother didn't comment, I doubt she had worn one for some time. Since I've known her, she has worn one then, one when we married and one when I took her to hospital to have the baby.

Rosemary rang the dinner bell. She rings it hard with long pauses in between, as if she's waiting for the sound to carry far up the hillside. Ralph shook my hand and went to wash up. Before he sat down, he drank off a small tumbler of whiskey. As if to apologize, he said, 'I allow myself that on a day like today.' His head was bare and white as an egg. The whiskey always relaxed him, making him slightly abstract. 'Well, it's here. It's been coming for weeks. We went through sixteen cords last winter. Not too bad. Fine parsnips, Mother.'

That made Rosemary smile and I'm certain I could actually feel a chill–the last vestige of winter–leave the room. The room actually became warmer. I didn't know it at the time, but the poached parsnips are a signal. Rosemary poaches parsnips once a year, on the day the thaw sets in.

'Yes. Mighty fine parsnips,' Ralph said again.

We ate quietly for a time. Then, Ralph set down his fork. 'The apples dropped this afternoon,' he said. 'They unfroze enough to drop. I was picking them up for the cows. Seemed like the branches were sort of grabbing at my hat and coat shoulders. Reaching down sort of. I'll be cutting them trees back some.'

'What on earth do you mean?' asked Rosemary. 'Ralph Burns, I don't know what you are talking about. That kind of talk isn't like you in the least.'

He sat up straight. His eyes took on a distanced look as if he were wrestling with a vague thought which he didn't know how to express completely. I understood only that something had happened to him in the orchard, something as forceful and unnerving as a vision of death. He seemed far away from us all sitting down there at his end of the long, food laden table. He seemed to be speaking across a great chasm. 'Trees,' he said, half to himself. 'It's them trees.' He bent over, hunching in his chair as if he were ducking, to show us what he meant. He supported himself with the chair's arms and looked at Rosemary with his head twisted sideways. 'I tell you, Mother, one day those apple trees are going to take a hold of my coat and throw me clean up . . .'

Rosemary held up her hand as if to push the words aside.

'That may sound strange, but I tell you it's not. I tell you that. Not to me, it's not . . .'

'Now, Ralph!' She was openly baffled and alarmed. She hid her concern by chiding him as if he were a boy. 'You hold that thought.' She worried her napkin over her lips. 'You eat your supper before it gets cold.'

'I have lived here for sixty-three winters. Sixty-three. And, Mother, my body is feeling it just now. That's what I'm saying.'

'You just take that idea right out of your mind,' she said.

'It's been sitting there. It's been sitting there like a crow for some time. I try tossing it off, Mother, but it won't toss. It's got itself hooked there. Its claws are stuck.'

The natural light in the room had faded. Rosemary excused herself and turned on the glaring overhead. In a quiet, but firm manner, she expressed her disappointment in her husband and urged him to pay attention to his supper. The girlish quality I had seen in her earlier was completely overtaken now by the strong and willful matron in Rosemary. She reminded him that we were all supposed to be celebrating the promise of the coming of spring, that it would be time to plant the corn and the garden soon, that soon there would be green vegetables for supper and not preserves, that it was no time to be talking about whatever it was he was talking about. Crows on his head.

Spread before us were the poached parsnips floating in a large white dish, mashed potatoes, creamed corn, stuffed pork chops with milk gravy. Yellows, light browns, whites. The pork chop stuffing was the same color as the earth which clings to the parsnips, rich and cold from the unfrozen garden.

'I know the thought is frightening,' he said, speaking intimately to her, as if Sarah and I weren't present. 'It comes to us all.'

'Eat!' she said. 'I want you to eat. We have company.'

'Obediently, he picked up a pork chop bone and directed his attention to his daughter. 'She tells me you've been in the river.'

'Yes, Papa. This afternoon.'

'Fine!' he said, cheered. 'That's fine. What a girl!'

'That's where I met Phillip,' she said. 'He thought I was trying to kill myself.' Looking across the table at me, she said, 'I wasn't.'

Her father disregarded both the remark and the warm smile she gave me. 'Careful,' he said. 'You should have on more clothes. You'll get a sore throat in that dress. I want your head good and dry before bed. It's not summer yet.' To me he said, 'You don't come from around here.'

'I have an apartment in Manchester,' I said, 'New Hampshire.'

When I told him what I was doing for work, Ralph said, 'I've never slept in one myself.' He pointed his thumb to the ceiling. 'Every night for more than forty years. I've got no use for them. You been out to that new one they set up south of town? They call it the Pine Edge. There aren't any pines within a mile of that place. I got no use for it.'

'You're lucky,' I said.

'What? Why do you say that?'

'No one wants to sleep there. They have to.'

'Well, all I know is my line of work doesn't require it.'

'That's what I mean.'

'Suppose so.'

After supper, Sarah and I tried sitting on the porch swing, but it was too cold. We moved inside to the parlor. She was silent for some time. 'Papa just acts like that sometimes,' she said, finally. 'Did he seem too strange to you?'

'Strange? Not really. Tired, yes.'

'He worries about being old and keeping this place going. He has arthritis.'

I had no response and kept quiet.

'He gets up at five every morning to milk. You understand, of course, he's going to need help someday. Either that or we'll have to give this place up.'

When I heard Ralph climbing the stairs for bed, I realized I should leave. Sarah's hair was not yet dry from her swim. I put my arm around her waist for a moment and felt her hips through the soft cloth of her dress. She leaned against me and I felt the moisture of her hair on my neck.

'You'll come back?' she asked. 'Promise me you will.' She turned her face upwards and looked at me. 'What do I have to do?'

I kissed her lightly.

'Again?' she whispered.

This time it was not a chaste kiss.

Then Sarah was watching me from the front porch as I sped down the valley. I sang along with the radio. At the bridge by Don Ketchum's garage, I gained speed. The car shook violently as it thundered over the bridge and slammed through the pot holes in front of Alice Cowper's small cottage. A wash of black water rose in the darkness and raked across the side of the building. In the mirror I saw a light go on. 'Sorry,' I yelled. 'I forgot the pot holes.'

In Sharps Crossing, I turned right at the First Congregational Church and, without stopping at the new motel nearby, went directly to Sharon and got on the Interstate. Two hours and a half later, I was lying flat on my back in my small apartment in Manchester unable to go to sleep.

After that first meeting, I began making frequent deliveries to the Pine Edge Motel in Sharps Crossing and to the Buena Vista in Sharon. Our courtship picked up its pace and fell into a rolling lope.

Her mother, who clearly understood Sarah's and my mutual attraction better, probably, than we did ourselves, realized she should learn something about my background and upbringing. Also, no doubt, the village gossips had begun to ask her questions about me which she could not answer. One evening she and I were sitting in the parlor after supper. Sarah had been asked to wash the dishes. Ralph was doing his bookkeeping upstairs.

'There now,' said Rosemary. 'I want to know about you.'

'Me? There's not much to say. I'm here.'

'Please begin,' she said, flashing me a smile. 'Anywhere you want.'

'I'm not very good on that subject.'

'Do you want some sherry or coffee or whiskey?'

I heard a chair scrape somewhere upstairs. Then, boots dropped onto the floor. A toilet flushed. I said I would prefer whiskey.

Unaccustomed to tending bar, Rosemary poured me a half a water glass full with no ice. And, in no time at all, my tongue was loose and my natural reserve was ambushed by the liquor.

'My mother and father are dead,' I said. 'They were killed in a skiing accident when I was young. My uncle raised me.'

'I'm sorry.'

'I was two at the time. My uncle was a fine man, a good father.'

'Where was this?'

'Uncle Lucas was a silver miner. We lived near Animas City, Colorado–that's in the Rocky Mountains. Originally, my mother was from Utah. My father came west from St. Louis. He was trained to be a geologist and got a job as a foreman on the day shift on a claim near Hatville, my mother's home town.

Uncle Lucas told me that after I was born, they would leave me sleeping in the bottom drawer of their bureau while they went off together on their army surplus skis which my father base waxed with melted down Victrola records–though that's hard to believe.'

'I can believe it,' Rosemary said. She got up and came to sit next to me on the couch. The cushions sagged and I took a big sip of the liquor.

'Those were the days, Mrs. Burns . . .'

She put her hand on my knee to stop me. 'Rosemary. I want you to call me Rosemary. We like you, Phillip. You take my daughter seriously. You do, don't you? We all like it when you visit.'

A flush rose to my cheeks. To cover my embarrassment, I said what I hadn't planned to say. 'Those were the days, the pre-hollow-ground-edge, the days of the stemmed Christy and bear trap bindings. Of silver paraffin . . .'

'At night? Your parents skiied at night? How could they see where they were going?' She removed her hand, but I could still feel its warmth and pressure.

'. . . days of Dick Durrance and Tony Matt, of the Stemmbogen and the Christiana. See where they were going? Oh, they used carbide lamps and miners' helmets. You know, those lamps toss a beam as strong as the brights on my car. I've used one.' I was still confused and embarrassed by her compliment and her closeness and went on. 'All of this was long before wedge turns and carving and chairlifts and the front Moebius flip, you understand. They walked up and skiied down.'

'What happened to them?'

'They just didn't come back to me. That's all I know–all I was told. They skiied away and Uncle Lucas lifted me out of the bureau drawer.'

'Poor you.' In sympathy, or what passed as sympathy, Rosemary touched my knee again.

'Oh, I was too young to feel anything. And Uncle Lucas took terrific care of me. He really did.'

'Anyway,' said Rosemary, standing up and smoothing her

dress. 'You're here now. It's good you're here. I want you to
know that we like you to come here and are grateful for the help
you give my husband with his work. We truly are.'
    She went upstairs then and I heard the bedroom door close.
At the time, I had no knowledge of snares or traps, specifically
the Havahart trap which captures small animals alive. 'It's a
nice way to go if you gotta go!' is the company's slogan. If it
sounded like anything, the sound of Rosemary's door closing
was trap-like, but instead of thinking about traps, bewildered
by flattery, I thought of a corral gate shutting and that I was a
stallion inside. And I didn't mind, at the time, I didn't mind
being corraled in the least. I fancied myself as Ralph Burns'
helper, his hired hand, though I worked for him without
pay.
    After Sarah finished the dishes, we talked–she would only let
us talk on the couch in the parlor because noises like rustling
clothing and heavy breathing pass easily through the floor of
the large bedroom upstairs. So that night Sarah was cool and
reserved. She wasn't interested at all in the pleasure I had from
talking with her mother. 'You don't talk to me like that,' she
said. We went to bed earlier than I wanted to and separate-
ly.
    A wind and rain storm had come up since supper. In my bed
at the back of the house, I listened to the storm come in up the
valley and cut across the chimney, flat across it, causing a small
fury inside the stove in my room. The door rattled and the little
wood burner shook. I lay wide awake and listened to the
storm–to its horizontal force–which was so unlike the quiet
vertical storms in the mountains of my youth. The whiskey had
made my head spin. To stop the motion, I put one foot on the
floor.
    My uncle and I lived in a four room cabin in the San Juan
Mountains, fifteen miles north and twenty-five hundred feet up
from Animas City. Uncle Lucas identified himself with a
number of professions–assayer, mining consultant,
prospector. Besides, he worked fitfully on his mining claim to
hold the rights. Even at sixty, which was his age when I came to
live with him, Lucas Tuttle could out scramble, out shoot, out

gopher and out *par*-lay (his term for fast talk by the coal stove) anyone except maybe Black Jack Johnson, who lived alone in an old Buick sedan down stream from us. Black Jack had removed the engine and replaced it with a sheepherder's stove. Evenings he and Uncle Lucas would open the car door on the driver's side and sit in lawn chairs talking.

After those fire and whiskey talks with Black Jack, Uncle Lucas would come home for supper. 'Decay,' Uncle Lucas told me many times as we sat across from one another on log benches. 'Death. Desolation. Phillip, you must learn to accept mutability in your life. The world will always change around you. People you love will die or go away. People you deeply need will turn against you. Still, as the world changes, it doesn't mean that your needs change one iota. Some needs, just like food, are elemental and immutable. Now, take me. You know damn well I like to be with people. I must have friends. We get plenty of that when the snow's gone, we get too much of it sometimes. That's why I talk to myself or to the furniture in winter. They keep me company. So? Let's say you have a favorite girl or dog. If either is taken away by accident or by death, you bet you are going to start looking for a replacement–tree, dog, or woman–as soon as your eyes are dry. Now, here's what I'm trying to say. You're the sort who needs a father. When you leave me, or when I leave you, you'll find a father in someone else. And, you'll continue looking and replacing fathers until you can stand alone. Then, all those fathers you've had will appear in your memory just as all of your girls will appear, like a single continuous ribbon of love or whatever you want to call it. That's the best advice I can give you. Don't let circumstance talk you out of your needs. Don't be ashamed by your needs. The old bitch nature is blind and ruthless and without mind, God love her. So, don't be afraid to accept substitutes–substitutes for me, even. In a pinch, I talk to the pans. How crazy or desperate is that? Go on, laugh at me you little smart ass. How would you like living with a cabin full of cats?'

As I lay in the small bedroom at the rear of the Burns' farm house, I couldn't remember how many times Uncle Lucas gave me that lecture, the same one. When Lucas finished, the room always seemed much larger to me–he made the world hold possibilities. Then, he would finish eating, letting it soak in. Stew, beans, split pea soup all tasted the same. Lucas stirred, seasoned, tasted, finally reducing the ingredients to a brown mass, all the time talking to the pans. One March, I remember, we ran out of carrots. Uncle Lucas used canned peaches instead. Neither of us could tell the difference.

Towards the end, my uncle slept more.

I sent word for a doctor, and he came up from Animas City by horse and snow shoes–a jeep would never have made it through. The doctor brought some sort of energy supplement which Lucas flatly refused to take.

'He's healthy enough,' the doctor told me, 'but he's losing his stamina. He's compensating–he's confused energy loss with contemplation.' The doctor left the medicine with me. When I tried to sneak some into the stew, Lucas said, 'Please Phillip. No.' He gently pushed the bowl away. 'I've not been in this condition before. I must accept it.'

'But the doctor . . .' I tried to force the spoon towards him. 'He said it would give you a jolt.'

'No jolts for me. Definitely no.' Lucas got out of bed and stood on the cabin stoop to urinate. His figure cut a dark silhouette in the mountainside, which rose almost vertically outside the cabin door. He returned to his room and wrapped himself in a thick blanket and sat on his bench at the table. His caved, congested chest was giving out. I got him a bowl of undoctored stew and waited until he had finished with it. All through the night, Lucas' breathing filled the cabin. It sounded like there was a rat walled inside, scraping his chest.

When Lucas died that winter, I put him in the ground with his miner's helmet, carbide lamp and prospector's pick, just as he wanted me to, sold the claim and cabin to Black Jack, and left the San Juan Mountains for good. I was eighteen. My years in the Coast Guard as a signalman have no place in this story, except to explain how an eighteen-year-old boy from Animas City, Colorado, could be seen, a man at twenty-two walking down the gang plank of a bouytender in Towlesport,

Massachusetts. On the day I was discharged, I wore civilian clothes and the boatswain piped me ashore. I was handed my papers and someone helped me shoulder my .heavy green duffle. The first thing I did was traditional. I got drunk with my old shipmates in a bar on Fish street and bought a car. Weeks later, I found myself in Manchester with the salesman job. The Mustang I now own is my second car. I had been with the motel supply company for three years when I met Sarah Burns.

As I closed my eyes, I listened to the piercing sheets of rain against the tin roof of the farm house. The sharp gusts seemed to misshape the room, turning the small sturdy rectangle into a parrallelogram. I thought once again of Uncle Lucas' lecture and somehow I knew that Ralph Burns would be my last father, that when the old bitch Nature took him away from me, or if accident did, it would be time to stand alone. The bursts of rain on the roof sounded like nails. I was here with one foot on the floor to prevent dizziness.

The following morning, she awoke me by tossing sticks up at the screen. I got out of bed and looked down at her standing ankle deep in the wet grass with her head thrown back and her neck arched. 'Phillip, the storm's over,' she whispered, sibilant in the soft morning light. 'It's a beautiful morning. Let's go to the quarry.' She wore her nightgown and bathrobe. 'Papa's the only one up. He's milking.'

I hurried down the back stairs carrying my shoes. The kitchen was empty. I followed her across the road and through the hay field, and we disappeared in the woods. There we took an old dirt road boardered by stone walls. The maples formed an arch way above us.

At the quarry, we removed our clothes together, inter-layering them in a single pile on a rock–my shoes, her robe, my trousers, her nightgown, my socks, my underwear. Together, we swam in the deep, clear quarry pool, and I dove under her and touched her goosefleshed legs and her back and her breasts. The early morning sun, and later, my hands and lips warmed and smoothed Sarah's flesh as we made love on the green moss that grows on the enormous blocks of marble at the edge of the abandoned quarry.

Like two, young, naive lovers with China doll eyes, we emerged from the woods hand in hand still wet from our swim in the fresh rain water. By that time, Ralph had finished milking and was crossing the yard with a jar of fresh cream. Robin Loomis had just stuffed the Sunday paper in the cylinder below the mail box and Ralph stopped to watch her pedal up the road. She is younger than Sarah and tartish. She wore a halter top and tight red shorts that made her bottom look like a bright red apple. When Ralph saw Sarah and I walking hand in hand across the hay field, he ducked and scurried into the house. I assumed he was embarrassed because we had caught him gazing at Robin Loomis.

We all were silent at breakfast. Though Sarah and I were flushed with pleasure, we couldn't look at one another. She put her bare feet on top of my shoes under the table and pretended to read the newspaper. I gazed into my plate of scrambled eggs and scrapple. The mood in the room was such that when the low toned bell from the church sounded for service, I thought first of death and then of nuptials.

That day, I helped Ralph, working hard right along with him. We didn't talk much. He gave me instructions in his flat, even voice. It was after supper that Ralph took me on a walk over the farm. We left the kitchen and crossed the yard to the barn. He went inside to check the bulk tank–temperature and level–and went to the bin for two buckets of pig feed. 'They'll eat as much as you give them,' he said. Ralph spoke in bursts when he was working. 'Once the ground loosens up. In late spring. They start right in' He sounded angry and condescending. 'You never saw pigs beat, I suppose.'

'No, Sir.'

'Once you get two of them alone, the old boy sets his feet and climbs on. I've seen him go for fifteen minutes. Feet. All six. Sunk in the yard muck. Look at her face sometime. It shows you how much she loves it.'

Ralph carried the two buckets of feed to the tractor cart and drove slowly up to the pig yard, which is a fair distance from the main house because of the smell. I followed the tractor.

From atop the wide steel seat of the old green Oliver, Ralph said, 'I haven't missed a feeding or a milking in forty-years. Once you start, it never stops, year after year. You're your own man as long as it doesn't start running you.'

'I see,' I said, though I didn't understand the half of it.

The pigs, their hind legs working furiously in the muck, were crowding the trough before Ralph had poured the feed. He stood back a distance and smiled at their nudging for a position. 'I love to watch them eat. They're hardly real animals. One hell of a lot smarter than cows.'

I have fed the pigs many times myself by now and have watched them beat. The act is soothing somehow. There is not the violence I had imagined there would be. And the sows aren't coy or protective, and her face does seem to gain an expression of pleasure, as if the act released her and rested her comfortable somewhere beyond the muck in the yard, possibly beyond the earth itself. Restful. At least, that's how my pigs seem to me.

We left the yard and walked to a point above the garden where we could look down on the main house and out-buildings. Ralph checked the current in the electric fence which surrounds the strawberries–'Hotcha! She's on.' The farm buildings, the house, the sheds and trees below us took resolve in the wide valley–a tight, ordered, almost completely self-contained world showed itself to me. 'There it is,' he said, 'all of it. It's my duty to keep it running right around the seasons. I was born in the red house below the bridge. The one across from Alice Cowper's.'

'The house with the pot holes,' I said.

'We sold that section off a few years back. I still hay that field and the one above it and the one across the road behind Ketchum's place, where you were this morning.'

That first mention of the morning stopped me. I had no idea how Ralph felt about that.

'My pa built the house we're in now when I was your age.' He laughed. 'Hell, you've come a damn site farther than I have. Three quarters of a mile in sixty-three years. And I don't expect to be going much further.'

We walked back to the tractor. Ralph told me to get into the seat. 'Let me show you how to run this thing.' As we bucked and lurched down the hill to the barn with Ralph balancing on the cart hitch, he said, 'I can't say I've got Sarah figured out. The first two daughters made it clear. Chicago and Houston. Sarah's more like me. She seems to want to stick here. At least she claims to.'

He taught me the clutch and the shifting. 'You learn quick,' he said. 'Hop down and let me take it into the shed.'

I followed him inside the tractor shed. Lordly up there on the seat, Ralph removed his blue and white striped engineer's cap. His head glowed. He looked hard at me, waiting for me to ask him what we both knew it was time for me to ask.

'I think a lot of Sarah, Sir,' I said.

'You best think more of her than that.'

'Well, I do.'

'How do you plan on supporting her?'

'Sir?' I had to yell over the belching engine.

'You'll work here. Come next spring, I want that girl right here. No carrying her off to some city someplace.'

'You mean? Of course, I promise. We'll both stay right here.'

As if the old tractor were relieved, it belched once more when Ralph killed the engine.

'Besides,' he said, 'If that girl doesn't get her dunk in the river each spring, she'll freeze up stiff on you.' He climbed down and we shook hands. 'Welcome. Now, let's go find her mother. From the way you two have been carrying on, her mother's got to wondering if you ever planned on making it legal.'

We walked towards the house together. 'Urges,' Ralph was saying. 'We all get them. Especially this time of year. Can't hide that. Well, no matter. I want to move into the hired hand's cottage. How soon can you make it? We've got corn to plant. From the looks of it we'll get two, maybe three, hay cuttings this year. Look for three.'

'I can quit on Monday,' I said, 'and be moved in two weeks from today.'

'Fine. Now, I want Sarah living over in the big house until

after the wedding. You might fix it up some for her. No one's lived there for a time. The water heater leaks. It could use some paint and the screens are rusted out.'

'Yes, Sir!'

'And you just as well start calling me Ralph. That's my name.'

'Yes, Sir . . . Ralph!'

I jumped when the screen door on the back porch snapped shut behind me. As I look at it now, it was as if the world had gotten suddenly quite small.

We were married early last June, and instead of going on a wedding trip, we stayed here to help Ralph hay the fields for the first of what was to be three cuttings—as Ralph had predicted. The Queen Anne's lace and the black-eyed Susans masked the hillside above the farm.

One day last August, while Ralph baled the small field behind the hired hand's cottage for the third time, I rested inside on the couch, waiting until it was time to go outside again in the humid heat and toss the endless string of bales into the truck. Sarah and Rosemary were stuffing sauage in the summer kitchen. From my position, I could see far up the hillside almost to the wood lot. Minutes passed. I could hear the baler motor and could visualize the golden bundles of hay easing out of the baler and falling haphazard onto the stubble. The barn was already full and we were filling sheds. It seemed to me that we had enough hay, but it didn't seem that way to Ralph.

'Phillip? Hey!' Ralph yelled to me from the kitchen. 'I've bunged my thumb on the twine cutter. Take me down to Tweet's for a stitch.'

My hands were raw and my back ached. I hobbled into the kitchen to find my father-in-law, who was letting the cut gush over the soaking breakfast dishes. Ralph pulled his freshly ironed, red bandana handkerchief out of the bib pocket of his overalls, and I wrapped his thumb.

'The cutter tripped on me,' he said. 'Damn fool. Call me a damn fool. I've got it coming.'

I told the old man that I didn't want to call him a damn fool.
'Well, I'm a fool anyway. Call me one. My God damn hands
don't work right anymore.'
'You are. All right? Ralph Burns, you're a God damn bloody
fool and a slave driver,' I said. The extraordinary intimacy I felt
with him made me add, 'And your damn foolish slave driving
blood is all over our dishes.'
'I believe I require a stitch.'
Aside from operating the only cafe in the village, Vernon
Tweet is the village vet as well. At one time or another, he has
sewn, shot or patched almost every man and animal in the
valley. He even helped Ven Loomis' wife give birth to her third
daughter and had jokingly offered to help Sarah with our first,
which was due that winter.
Tweet, a short man with enormous hands, cleared away the
condiments on the counter top and began to sew. While we
were there, Robin Loomis, the paper girl, came in to buy a
Snickers chocolate bar. She wore a scant two piece bathing
suit, no shoes, and was pressing a red ball against her hip. I
rung up the sale, because Tweet was scrubbed down and rubber-
gloved. Ralph looked up from his wound, but when she went to
him, he quickly diverted his gaze.
'You're hurt, Mr. Burns,' she said, standing close, almost
touching him, leaning over his arm to look at his thumb. The
top of her bathing suit drooped and you could see between her
breasts the downy hair on her belly. Ralph didn't seem to know
where to look. So, he fixed his gaze on the catsup bottle at the
far end of the counter. Robin smelled of sun tan oil and her
nudity and her youth made his face turn color.
'No, It's nothing. I'm a damn fool,' he said.
'You are nothing of the kind,' she said.
Aside from his blush, I think there was something else,
something behind the coloring on the old man's face. He
blushed from habit. All Ralph wanted, as far as I could tell, was
to have his thumb repaired and to get back to haying, away
from the untouchable reality of her presence, back to day
dreaming as he worked. I suppose that comes to all of us,
sooner or later, whether we want it to come to us or not. At

least, Tweet and I watched Robin walk out of the cafe. 'Ain't she something?' Tweet said, and I nodded, agreeing. 'This time last year she was skinnier than a pole bean.' Ralph's single-mindedness made me feel stupid laughing at Tweet's joke. An embarrassment swept over us, and we all applied our attention to Ralph's cut and spoke of other matters, avoiding talk about Robin Loomis, who had suddenly become more of a dirty joke than a young girl. But, how can you blame a man who knows his time is almost gone? There must come a time when you don't want a jolt any longer, because you know it won't last and won't prolong anything.

Patched now, his thumb a white flag on the tractor's steering wheel, Ralph finished the baling. When the truck rumbled up behind the hired hand's cottage, I was up in the bathroom considering, among other things, how pleasant it would be to be spending the afternoon somewhere other than down in the field tossing bales into the truck.

The gentle hills surrounding this farm, curved and almost feminine, hold no trace of ruggedness or inassailability. There are no magnificent nor awesome mysteries here, but a conglomerate of small ones–a stand of poplars, a sink hole with a bog, the moss bed up by the ledges, the quarry pool, the massive mother oak growing out of the cellar hole up in the wood lot. Nothing here approaches the sublime, towering peaks of the San Juan Mountains to which I am accustomed–gazing at them, as I once did, while I sat on the privy behind Uncle Lucas' cabin. The raw, brutal mountains of my youth have no part in a dairy farmer's routine. And, I am now a dairy farmer. I run this place alone. Quite simply, circumstances are such that milk has become my concern now and not mountains.

From the bathroom, I looked down and saw Ralph standing in the center of the field with his hands on his hips. The smell from the pig yard came in through the screen on the bathroom window.

'Working hard? Hey!' I'm ready to load up when you are,' he yelled up to me.

I flushed and went down to toss bales. Sarah drove the truck.

Ralph stayed up in the bed stacking. My job was the most exhausting. When Ralph saw how pale I was and that I had begun to stagger under the effort, he got out the lemonade. 'You're out of shape,' he said.

I had stopped sweating, though the day was a hot one, and my skin was dry and my face burned. Fearing heat stroke (and the loss of a good, unpaid worker) Ralph asked me to drive to town for more baling twine, claiming it was cheaper to pick it up in White River Junction than in the village at Ven & Lou's store.

'That's not true,' I said, 'not if you count gas.'

'Go anyway. You need the time.'

As I was leaving, Rosemary, who had finished the sausage by herself and was now weeding the garden, left her work and ran lightly down the drive. 'Wait,' she called. 'I want to go with you.'

She changed her clothes and came out of the house carrying two small jars of strawberry preserves and a package of meat–payment for Tweet's doctoring.

Sarah, from the field, tooted the truck's horn. 'Have fun you two. Be good.' she said.

So, Rosemary and I left them. Daughter was driving the truck in slow circles over the stubble; Father was tossing bales one-handed onto the flat bed.

Once we were through the village and on the road to White River, I noticed the pleasant odor of Rosemary's perfume.

'Ralph's going to kill me,' she said, touching my arm. 'But I'm bringing home a leg of lamb. When I was a girl, we always had roast lamb when the sweet corn was ready. There's nothing quite like it.'

Though I feel warm and intimate with Rosemary, though she can ignore the difference in our ages and can peel the years away at will, though her affection and her impulse are genuine, I still didn't know what I was supposed to do or say.

In white River, I drove diagonally across the shopping mall's huge blacktopped parking surface and found a slot near the hardware store. I locked the car and went for the twine, while

Rosemary went into the women's shop next door.

I was loading the twine in the trunk, when she came out in a bright silk sunfrock. It was low at the bodice and lifted her breasts, which are considerably fuller than Sarah's are. She had a new scarf on her head. Half way to the meat store, she realized she was still carrying the tote bag which held her faded calico dress, and she ran, quite literally sprinted, back to the car to deposit it. Though she is in her mid-forties, she provoked in me such a vision of youthfulness and enthusiasm that I found it difficult to believe that she was actually my mother-in-law and the wife of a sixty-three-year-old farmer. Breathing hard, she took my arm and we walked along the plate-glass promenade, past Sears and Finast, and into the sawdust and air conditioning of Rebozo's Meat Market.

On the way home, the car once again filled with the odor of her perfume. The leg of lamb, wrapped in white, was between us on the car's seat. Instead of taking the Interstate to Sharon, I got onto Route Fourteen, which follows the White River.

'I'm enjoying myself,' she said. 'Are you?'

'I like your dress. I've never seen you dressed up.'

'Does it fit? Do you think it's too little . . . skimpy up front?'

'Oh no, not that.'

Then, we were quiet for a time. Rosemary looked out of her window. I reached to turn on the radio, but decided against it without really knowing why. I was pulled towards her, attracted towards her, but she seemed silly, somehow, cheap, too. It was obvious she wanted me to admire her. But, I think, she wanted more. At least, that afternoon, I thought she was anticipating an advance from me–a hand on her leg, something. Certainly, she would pary such intimacy from me, but at the same time I know she would have taken deep satisfaction in my approaching her if only to be able to push me away. Show me you want me, then I'll say no.

I looked at her briefly, at her bare throat and her scarf. She was a beautiful and a desirable woman.

'There,' she said. 'There's a place. Let's stop for just a minute. I feel like I never really get away.'

She left her shoes in the car and ran to the river bank to

wade. I found a grassy spot where she joined me. She raised her dress above her knees, legs firm and strong, and leaned back resting on her elbows enchanted by the motion and sparkle of the current.

She caught me looking at her. Her amazing, pale gray-blue eyes held mine for a moment. The vain, girlish side to her character seemed to increase, and I found myself forgetting her other self–the woman I knew she was, Sarah's mother, who always wore a faded calico dress and a fresh white apron, who always washed the kitchen floor after breakfast and again just before supper. She looked more like the young girl in the photograph on the soap stone stove in the parlor then.

Something in our eyes made us break our gaze. Now, when Rosemary spoke, I found myself unable to ignore her legs and the sun on the fullness of her breasts. 'You have no idea,' she said. 'What a help you are to Ralph. No. I really mean it. I do.' She was not saying what her body told me.

The river passed by slowly. The subtle eddies, rising and swirling were just perceptible. She removed her scarf and shook her dark hair. Once more, traces of flirt and girlishness cancelled her age and I felt stirrings of desire. 'I want you to tell me, Phillip, tell me exactly how you feel about me.'

'Me? Tell about you?' I wanted to slap her for what she was doing to me. I couldn't look at her. I didn't know which side of her I wanted to see or which side of her was genuine. It was a question of calico or silk. 'I love you,' I said, which was true no matter what she wore.

Her cheeks colored. She touched my arm gently and tossed back her head. 'Well, I love you too,' she said. Her tone of voice was hard, challenging, almost mean.

'If you mean do I think of you as Sarah's mother or as something else, I'll tell you,' I said.

'I think I know,' she said. And, she did, for the girlishness vanished.

The late sun enhanced the deep, rich color of the river. I left her alone and walked towards a stand of poplars which opened onto a small grassy clearing. I passed a black sedan and began to climb up the flood bank of the river. Once over the steep lip, the path flattened out somewhat into an oblong meadow which swelled with grass and full bushes of deep and luxuriant green. The sun was strong and hot away from the river. I didn't know why I had asked her that, so pointedly, but I was terribly relieved that I had had the courage to.

A youth was sitting on a rock close to the path. I smelled the boy's cigarette an instant before he turned and saw me. A hat covered the boy's lap. He wore no shirt.

'Hallo,' I said. A group of starlings lifted off the nearby bushes.

'I wouldn't go no further, if I were you.' The boy's words, which held no threat, were nothing more than a territorial warning and they stopped me as effectively as a knife. The youth had an anticipatory edginess about him, a nervousness, a colt-like unpredictibility that made him dangerous. 'You wouldn't want to interrupt.'

'Right,' I said, certain now that he had a knife under his hat.

I turned around and went back into the shelter of the poplar trees. Over my shoulder, I heard another voice, and looked back through the trees to see a second youth, who had his chest puffed out, buckling his trousers. He sat down on the rock and laughed as the first boy disappeared at a half-run up the trail. The puffed-up one found the half smoked cigarette, cocked back his head and blew a thin stream of smoke into the sky as if to provoke the clouds into combat.

Rosemary's new dress blended with the leaves and grass. Still supporting herself on her elbows, she faced the last of the sun. She didn't hear me approach, and I crept up behind her and covered her eyes with my hands.

'Of course, you're right, she said. 'I'm so silly sometimes. Still, it's lovely here with you. We should come back here again sometime, all the same.'

'I think we should go now. We're not exactly alone.'

She lifted her hand and I helped her up. Her knees were stiff. She looked as if every joint in her body ached. The girlishness had completely disappeared and she took neither my arm nor my hand as we walked back to the car.

It was almost dusk when we arrived back at the farm. 'I'm going in by the front,' she said. 'This dress is meant to be a surprise.' Clutching the leg of lamb under one arm and her tote bag under the other, she walked slowly up the front porch steps.

I sat for a moment staring after her. Then, I noticed that the picnic table had been butted against the large sugar maple at the side of the house. Someone had spread a red calico tablecloth over the weathered boards and set out kerosene lanterns.

Sarah came out of the summer kitchen with a large tray. Her slow movement told me that she had exhausted herself haying. She distributed the stainless, the tin cups, and the blue and white enamel plates as if she were slow dealing cards. A freshly killed chicken smoked on the outdoor grill.

When I honked the car's horn, Sarah flinched, clattering the plates. I waved out the window, trying to cheer her up. 'Say there! Hello, Ma'am. You got a real nice place here. Don't need a hired hand, do ya? I'm no farmer, but I'd learn real quick bein' next to a woman the like of you.'

'Learn to goof off, you mean.'

My kiss grazed her cheek. 'I didn't realize we were gone so long.'

'Four hours to go to White River? Papa's dead tired. He made me hold supper. We finished all the upper field and he did the milking. What took so long?'

'Your mother shopped. You should see her new dress. It makes her look your age. Don't mention it. She's keeping it a secret, a surprise for your father. After that we stopped by the river. You know, the time just sort of disappeared.'

'I'll bet it did. I'll bet you told her everything. I know you did! I wanted to be the one to tell her. I was going to tonight.'

'I did not. Besides, they must know anyway.' I stepped backwards. 'It shows from the way you act, even if there's no bulge yet.'

Instinctively, her hands covered her belly.

I went to the grill. 'May I turn the chicken?'

The plate she was holding shot across the picnic table,

bounced once and landed in the grass. 'You will not touch that chicken!' She hunched her shoulders and wiggled her head from side to side like an upset goose. 'You don't care. Do you? You haven't the slightest interest in . . . in . . . me, in this. You don't. I know now you don't.'

I laughed. Well, she looked so ridiculous.

She turned away, stood frozen for a moment and ran up the road toward the pig yard.

I sort of jogged behind her. When I apologized for laughing at her and tried to take her hand, she shook herself free. 'Please don't touch me. I don't want you to touch me just now. And I'm too tired to fight.'

'I didn't mean . . . I'm sorry.'

'You're sorry. Sorry for what? You haven't done anything to be sorry for. Except by not doing anything at all. We don't have enough cash to pay for the doctor or the delivery room. What are you doing about that? What if something goes wrong? What have you done about that?'

I held up my hand like a school crossing guard to stop her flow of words. 'Also, you haven't mentioned that you will need a washing machine,' I said. 'What have I done about that?'

'I don't want to do diapers in the public machine. It isn't sanitary.' Her anger had calmed somewhat. She felt she was justified. She felt on firm ground in her uncomplicated and exhilirating pure, white fury which raged through her. She had been holding back her discontent and her worry for days and days. Now, she could focus it directly and with relentless and fierce certitude, knowing I had no defense. Rosemary and I had goofed off for too long.

When I tried to touch her again, to assure her that her belief that I was indifferent was not true, she ducked away. 'To think,' she said, 'I'm carrying your child. Sometimes I wish I weren't.'

I began to walk away. Her blundering lack of faith in my reserve disappointed me. I didn't want to become spiteful, but a new found and deep emotion registered itself then. It was Sarah who wanted the child to begin with, Sarah who had conveniently not protected herself from the beginning, from that morning at the old quarry where it probably happened. Then, the day after we were married, it was Sarah who sprang the news of her pregnancy on me like the news was a catamount jumping me from from a tree limb. It was Sarah who was proud she hadn't had a period since May. It was Sarah who kept it a secret because she believed I would not have married her if I had known. The disappointment built with equal ruthlessness as had her fury. I tried to tell her carefully, deliberately, precisely, after our wedding night, that I felt no need for children just yet, that the farm would be enough to worry about for now, that we should plan on taking it over one day, that I wanted to live with her, just her, for a while, then she said, 'It won't be for long,' and covered her belly. I wished I had stayed on the farm and hayed. Then, if I had, if she had raged at me, then I would have been too exhausted to care. I crossed the yard to the picnic table where her parents sat waiting for us to finish yelling at each other. They held themselves erect, stiff, as if they were willing themselves properly deaf. I'm sure they heard us. If they heard only scattered phrases, the tone of the yelling revealed enough.

Rosemary had changed out of her new dress and now wore a faded calico. The afternoon's sun had put a glow on her cheeks and she smiled at me, openly and with understanding. There was no trace of girlishness or flirtation now, and there would not be again.

'I believe I should eat in the house,' I said. 'Excuse me.'

'Suit yourself,' said Ralph.

While I was serving myself, Sarah joined her parents at the table. She was still fuming mad and kept her back towards me until I was inside our house. Through the open window, I heard her break the news to them in a half-whine, half-angry tone, which was followed by a thrill of delight from Rosemary.

'It may be wonderful,' said Sarah, 'but he doesn't think so.' And she burst into tears.

'Now, come now. Quiet, Sarah. Listen. Of course, he wants it. Anyone can see that. Don't cry. We can all see that. You're just tired, that's all. Quiet now. Don't cry. We can all see that. You're just tired, that's all. Quiet now. Don't worry my darling.

It's absolutely wonderful news. Ralph, give her your handkerchief. Here now. That's the girl. Eat something. We'll talk after supper. You and I. We'll talk all about it. That's my darling.'

A vague remorse filled me. By the time I had finished my plate of cold baked beans, potato salad and chicken it was dark. A while later, Ralph knocked tentatively on the screen door; 'How do, father-to-be? Got a cup of coffee? The women have locked me out of the house.'

'There's some instant. I have whiskey if you want that.'

'Instant's fine,' said Ralph. 'You take the whiskey. Hell, you deserve it. Let's sit on the porch.' He patted my shoulder. 'By Glory, it's too glum indoors.'

We settled ourselves on the porch swing. Ralph didn't look at me directly. Instead, he squinted at the lights from Ketchum's living room across the road. 'I've got to say, everything aside, I'm awful damned pleased and hope it's a boy,' said Ralph.

'I am too,' I said. To Ralph, maybe to Ralph alone, could I admit to the fact I was proud. 'But, I don't care what it is.'

'Well, I guess it don't matter. I've lived with women. When I was your age, there were four of them in the house with me, the wife and three daughters. Have yourself a son first and then a couple of girls. There's no need for more than that.'

Aside from Ralph's slow, friendly voice, I could hear nothing but the far away rush of the river, and the breeze in the sugar maple at the side of the big house and the creaking of the swing chains as Ralph, unconsciously, pumped it for us both.

'You get in bed with them and it's bound to happen,' Ralph was saying. He pumped the swing higher than I usually do, and I let Ralph do the swinging. He worked the porch swing the way he worked everything in his life, and I wondered briefly if there ever had been a time in the old farmer's life when he was not confined, mechanical and almost mindlessly vigorous. I wondered if there ever had been a time in his life when he had felt as clean and as fresh and as impenetrable as–well, as a young boy, his passions sated, blowing smoke defianately at the sky.

'We'll bale the upper field tomorrow after breakfast,' Ralph said. 'That'll take until noon. I'll give you the rest of the day off. Take Sarah on a picnic or something. Ask her. She'll go with you. Who milks tomorrow?'

'It's your turn.' I stopped the swing. 'No. You took my place tonight. I milk tomorrow.'

Ralph congratulated me again, then he disappeared into the barn to check the cows and the temperature in the milk vat. I wouldn't be surprised to know that Ralph passed the news of his impending grandfatherhood along to each of his cows, one by one—Bessie, Dot, Frances, Hilda, Jane, and so on down the line, not leaving out any one of them.

I sat in the swing a while longer. Ralph cut the lights. The noise of the barn door swinging closed startled the pair of nesting swallows off the huge copper weather vane on top of the utility shed, sending the birds crying and confused into the night.

When the nights became chilly, in mid-November, Sarah and I moved out of the cottage and across the yard into the big house. Originally, we planned to live there only for the winter.

Sarah and I took over the master bedroom above the parlor. Ralph and Rosemary moved into the small guest room above the kitchen at the back of the house, where I used to sleep when I first came here as Sarah's beau.

On our first night in the big house, I sat alone in the parlor in the green patent rocker, waiting for the mouse traps to spring. I had them set throughout the dining room, kitchen and pantry to eliminate the mice before they had a chance to store up winter supplies and build nests in the walls. For years, Rosemary had handled the mousing herself, getting up throughout the night to reset the traps. She claimed she could wipe out an entire colony in three nights. I decided to remain in the arena of the slaughter and took up my position in the green rocker armed with one of Ralph's long flashlights.

A snap went in the kitchen. I followed the torch beam and righted the trap. I raised the spring, letting the limp, limp-tailed, rodent drop into a paper bag with his relatives–brothers, sisters, aunts. I carried the cheese in my bathrobe pocket.

As the night progressed, I noticed that they were getting smaller. Could they have had a seniority system? Did they send the youngest out last? A miniature, but unmistakable, atmosphere of the battlefield hung in the house that night as I waited in the green rocker—feet off the floor—for the traps to go.

Well, Philip, I said to myself. Here you are. What's going to happen to you now? He's made you the farmer here. You're the farmer on this place. So, what's now? Here you are, my boy. A farmer for the rest of your life.

Rosemary and Ralph were out at the church dance and supper. Sarah was asleep. Except for her remarkably sonorous snores and the irregular punctuation of the traps popping in various corners of the house, it was quiet.

The day before, as the sun was setting, Ralph had fired six shots in rapid succession from up in the wood lot above the farm. His signal cut through the silence of the valley. Rosemary stepped out of the house and responded by ringing the dinner bell. Sarah whistled from the garden where she was turning under the last of the peppers and eggplants. I stopped splitting chunk wood and went to Rosemary.

'He's got his deer,' she said.

'I'll go up after him,' I said.

Pulling the cart behind the old green Oliver, I drove past the garden, waved to Sarah and climbed the steep road up into the hills beyond the upper field.

Ralph was sitting slumped over on a campstool in the dim woods. He wore his blue and white striped overalls, gumboots, and striped engineer's cap with a red bandana pinned to the crown. The shiny thirty-thirty Winchester in his lap looked misplaced, as if it had been left by a passing hunter. He didn't look up at the sound of the tractor and continued to sit motionless at the fork of two game trails, a spot he had used for more than twenty-five years to get his deer on the first day of the season. Himself, he didn't favor venison, but it cost him no more than the price of the bullets. Besides, Rosemary truly relishes the delicate liver of the animal.

'She's dead,' he said, handing me his hunting knife. The sun was almost gone. The doe's head was not ten feet from his gumboots. She had been hit twice–once in the right foreleg, breaking it, once from the front near the heart. The emerging slug had exploded a section of the doe's spine. 'I needed all six this year,' he said. 'She was on top of me. I thought she'd never go down. I can't see so well in this light to hit clean the way I used to. It's dangerous for me to be up here. I was a damn fool to come.'

I stood with my hands hung at my sides uncertain (not wanting to be certain) what he intended for me to do.

'Take the knife,' he said. 'My hands are stiff. You take it from here. I'm tired.'

I took the knife and walked across the carpet of cold leaves to the fallen doe.

'Slit the throat first. Then, raise her head high and pump some out. Take the back legs and push more out. Watch for the two glands below the hocks. Musk. Spoils the meat.'

The animal's eyes held me and did not flinch or focus even when I punctured the skin at her throat and found the slippery jugular and severed it. Her blood was faintly warm and startled my hands, which were no longer part of me as they followed the old man's instructions. I lifted her head and pumped some out. I pumped out still more with her hind legs.

'Rest her head and shoulder against that log,' he said. 'Spread her legs. Cut around the anus and pull out six inches of gut and squeeze out the stool.' His voice was without modulation. It was the same tone of voice Ralph had used time after time while instructing me how to load twine in the baler, how to run the tractor, how to stack hay, how to work the old milker, how to soothe a cow in pain and help her along with her calf. 'Tie a knot. If you feel sick, breathe. Breathe deep through your nose and count. You'll get used to it.'

I had expected a soft stool. When half a dozen pellets fell onto the brilliant leaves, I said aloud, 'Deer shit! Real deer shit!'

My hands were my own again and worked smoothly in the fast diminishing light. I slit and I cut, following the drone of

Ralph's voice. I lay her on her side and let her belly and guts roll onto the leaves, loose and steaming. I reached in blind to pull out her lungs. I opened her chest cavity, parting her ribs at the end and rolled her over onto her belly to drain off her fluids. Then, I dragged her up to the tractor cart.

When Ralph stood, the forgotten rifle clattered to the ground. He helped me load her into the cart. Then, hunched like a gnome, he went to the mound of innards which were still steaming in the leaves, found what he wanted and wrapped it in his red bandana.

I drove us out of the dim wood lot and down the road to the farm. Ralph sat in the cart on the doe's shoulder. 'Rosemary likes the liver,' he said, as we clattered down the road by the barn. 'Bring it to her. Always.'

We lifted the animal onto the meat hook in the utility shed and covered her with cheese cloth. 'You plan on doing the shooting next year,' said Ralph. 'That was too close for me. From the amount of work you do around here, it's only right that you be called the farmer from now on. I'm no good anymore. No better than the green-horn you were when you first came here.'

So, before Ralph and Rosemary left for the church supper and dance the next evening, without hesitation or remorse, Ralph declared before Sarah and Rosemary that I was now the farmer on this place and was to be treated as such, that from then on he would supervise as best he could, health permitting, and show me how to manage the accounts. 'The boy's going to be a good farmer,' he said to them. 'This place is in good hands. He does a damn sight better than I did at his age. I'm kicking myself upstairs.'

'Oh, thank you, Papa,' said Sarah. 'It's because you taught him.'

'Though we seldom partake,' said Ralph, 'I'd like a whiskey before we go out. To celebrate my retirement. I bet Philip would too.'

He filled our glasses and looked at me. Assuming he expected some sort of acknowledgement, I raised my glass high. 'To the cows. To our eleven staunch and faithful milkers

out there ruminating in the barn. To cash flow.'
'That's the spirit,' said Ralph. 'Who milks tomorrow?'
'I say you milk. I say it's your turn. Now, be home early.'
'Oh, go on with you,' said Rosemary. 'You know we always are.'

Sarah and I ate supper, and she went up to bed immediately afterwards leaving me with the traps.

Another one went about eight-thirty. The mouse was not as large as my thumb, discounting the tail, and had been caught along the back, as if he had been running across the floor and had triggered the spring without the help of the bait. Or else, I imagined as I let him drop into the paper bag with his dead kin, or else, in despair, realizing he was alone, he had flung himself onto the bait tray to die.

That night with Ralph and Rosemary gone, the responsibility Ralph had passed along to me sunk in. I felt that I may be a victim in some larger design. Were the three of them–yes, I could include Sarah in this scheme, too–so desperate to preserve this farm? Had I been gently coerced into making my life here, into working like a fool and breeding children? It is cynical and cruel to say it, but I believe our child will, in her turn, snare her man out of the village or off the road, as I was snared, and move him into the hired hand's cottage to wait until it is time to take over the master bedroom in the main house from Sarah and I. In my bones, I know one of our children will follow Sarah and I into the rear bedroom to die. It began today when Sarah took Christy, our daughter, down to the Ompompanoosuc for a dip. If Christy doesn't want to stay here, to become resolutely tied to this farm, then one of our children will, and Sarah and I will love that one the best, for by doing so the child will become us. The perversely fated form of our lives rose up green and slick that night in the dark house with the traps, and it shames me now to see it so clearly, but I cannot escape. I am a farmer for the rest of my life. And my heart, just as Ralph's heart was, will become as tight and as hard and as unrelenting as an old berry root when I die in the back bedroom.

That night, while the traps fired, I sat in the patent rocker, and for the first time in months, I drank. It had begun to rain. The brilliant red and purple leaves were stripped from the sugar maple by the rain. I sat in the pitch black parlor and I got stinking drunk, because, after all, when you suddenly see your life all laid out for you, like a bolt of calico, when there doesn't seem to be any general source for suspense or chance remaining, when you understand there are only daily uncertainties, it makes you feel old, old and almost as good as dead.

As always, the whiskey wasn't any help. I let the flashlight drop to the parlor floor and ate the rest of the cheese from my bathrobe pocket. By ten, I was almost completely lubricated. The car lights in the driveway and their laughter sent me upstairs where I fell onto the bed. I didn't bother with my clothes.

'I got the whole damn family,' I whispered to Sarah, who stirred slightly when I lurched into a sitting position to take off my shoes. 'Every one of them, every single one.'

The following morning, Ralph coldn't get out of bed, and I milked the cows with a hangover. Rosemary took the news calmly and, a few days later, drove the old man to the hospital in Hanover. He lasted three weeks. Rosemary accepted his death the way she accepted the passing of the season. Sarah had to be put to bed. And the cows, sensing the old man's absence, reduced their production. Except for Jane and Nanci, all of them cut down to less than ten pounds a day. When Ralph's Bessie dropped to seven, I considered drying her off. But, it seemed uncharitable to pull Ralph's favorite just then, and I kept her on the line.

Myopic and quiet, the winter began. I boarded up the hired hand's cottage, and the cold closed in around us. Sarah was due in Feburary, and her belly had grown full. During the day she wore red suspenders and had to leave her trousers' fly half open. I hadn't noticed how full she was until one evening I saw her in her bathrobe, the cord tied above the bulge. She was enormous. 'I'll paint the nursery tomorrow,' I said.

I looked older now, dressed as Ralph used to dress–striped

overalls and a striped cap. Two of my cows calved earlier in the winter, and I was able to handle that alone. Still, I miss the old man. I don't know how many times I have got to the barn late in the morning half expecting that Ralph would be there before me, preparing the milking machine.

At meals, no one sits at the head of the table. We find ourselves looking down at his empty chair. At times, Sarah, forgetting, sets a fourth place at the table. Finally, this afternoon, Rosemary asked Sarah and I to sit at the head and foot. 'After all,' she said, 'soon my grandchild will be big enough to sit across from me.'

On the fifteenth of February, Sarah packed her suitcase, to be ready. A few days later she was awakened by a tightening which frightened her. At breakfast, she told us she felt fine, but that it was coming. The following evening, trying to distract myself with the account books, I heard Rosemary. 'They're at twenty minutes,' she called up to me, 'I think you should take her.'

I changed clothes and found Sarah in the back seat of the car clutching her suitcase.

I drove slowly through the empty village.

'Hurry,' she said, 'I don't want anyone to see me like this.'

In the rear view mirror, I saw her white face. It stiffened.

'Oh boy! Oh, my God! It hurts!' She breathed. 'I didn't think it would hurt this much.'

We probably should have made a dry run to the hospital because I couldn't locate the entrance. Leaving Sarah with gritted teeth in the parking lot, I searched the building for an open door. After all, birth is a natural occurance, not an emergency. So, I tried all the normal entrances, which were all locked at that hour. After making a complete circuit of the building–over rock walls and through shrub beds covered with drifted snow–I found the emergency entrance. As I vaulted a brick planter and burst into the building, I saw the nurse on duty wheel Sarah away to Maternity. My shoes were filled with snow and I'd ripped my jacket on something.

The doctor lived just down the street. Though the bag hadn't burst, the nurse thought it wise to call. I helped her move Sarah from the labor table onto a rolling stretcher. The halls were quiet. No one else seemed to be having babies that night. The Delivery Room had the appearance of being old and unused. Frances, the assisting nurse whose glasses kept sliding down her nose, went quickly around the room turning things on. The overhead. The incubator. She checked the oxygen mask. We transfered Sarah onto the delivery table. She seemed to have gained weight. The hard contractions began almost immediately.

'Try not to push,' said the nurse. 'Doctor will be here any minute.'

'I'm not sure I can hold back.'

A panic bolted through my belly. 'Can you do it?'

Sarah squeezed my hands against the pain, driving a fingernail into my palm, cutting.

'I haven't done it for a long time,' said Frances. She spoke calmly. Even as she spoke, I saw that she was remembering, ticking off a list of precautions which she had learned once by heart. Her coolness immediately dissolved my panic. And, a moment later, the sweet inevitability of nature took over.

'Now,' said Frances, 'I want you to push the next time. I want you to push harder than you have ever pushed in your life.'

Sarah lurched to one side and I pinned her shoulders to the table, afraid she would fall off. She cried out.

Frances pushed her glasses up her nose again. 'Go ahead and swear, if you have to, dear. But, push. Push hard. It won't come by itself.'

Sarah worked hard, forcing herself, somehow, to overcome the pain. Frances watched carefully until it was time to receive the head, but she did not pull. She lifted slightly to allow for a smooth passage, checking the cord. Then Sarah lapsed into two quick contractions. She was pushing so well by that time and the contractions were so strong that it seemed to me that our daughter was literally propelled from Sarah's body. 'It must be huge,' Sarah gasped afterwards.

Frances rested our daughter in the incubator, and I stood for I don't know how long looking into her eyes. It seemed to me that a spark of love traveled between us. I don't know what else it could have been–a glance of recognition.

None of us saw the doctor, who was standing by the door. 'Well,' he said, 'it looks like you didn't need me at all. That was quite something, young lady. Congratulations.' Frances was wiping Sarah's face. 'I can't thank you enough,' Sarah said. 'You were really terrific. I can't tell you.' 'Goodness, don't thank me,' said the nurse. 'You've given me the best night I've had in ages.'

As I drove back to the farm, smoking a cigar, I realized that I was still numb from excitement. Numb and so thoroughly amazed that I had forgotten to turn in my green smock and cap and shoe covers. I thought it would be like calving and had not anticipated her pain nor had I imagined that Sarah had such courage. So that's why. So that's why she has acted the way she has. So removed from me. She was getting ready. Then I remembered how tired she looked when I left her, but how serene and beautiful she had become during her term and was glad I had a physical memory of her pain. When she squeezed my hand during one of the contractions, her fingernail had cut into my palm.

It's hard to believe that it's spring again, that there's a squawling baby in the house, that in a month it will be our first wedding anniversary. This past winter has been as long and as hard as anyone in the valley can remember. According to my calender in the milking room, the first snow fell on the twentieth of November. Now, in mid-May, it's all but gone. There's still a pile at the north side of the house by the bulkhead and a few patches are left on the hillside. We didn't run out of wood, but went through almost eighteen cords. The maple sap has stopped flowing, the buds are out, and the river has been running high and brown for almost four days.

After milking this morning, I dug the parsnips, just like Ralph did every year before this one. I took a couple in for Rosemary. When I handed them to her, she pulled her house coat closed tight at her throat.

'Oh! I'd almost forgotten,' she said. Her eyes looked tired. 'So, Phillip, you've dug them this year?'

I think–no, I'm certain–there was a catch in her voice.
'He used to bring me ones just the same,' she said.
'I know he did. I hope you don't mind if I do.'
She shook her head, and I couldn't look at her anymore.
Earlier, about three o'clock, I drove Sarah down to the bridge. On purpose, I stopped at the same place I had a year ago, the place where I had first seen her. Sarah took off her clothes and carefully submerged herself in the swift brown water, while I held our daughter. Sarah didn't feel confident enough to swim this year, for certain she will next and the year after that. I must say, I was surprised by her thinness and by the fullness of her milk-filled breasts as the brown water coarsed over her. She stayed in the water for only a minute or two, fulfilling, I imagine, her promise to herself as much as hers to her father. Then, I helped her up the steep bank to the bridge and we drove back to the farm.

I've finished the evening milking now, and it's just about time for me to go in and wash up for supper. Poached parsnips floating in butter and cream, buttered creamed corn, stuffed pork chops with milk gravy and mashed potatoes flecked with black pepper. I can count on it. There will be no green vegetables on the table.

There goes the supper bell.

Sarah always rings it with short rapid strokes.

It's up to me now. I must sit at the head of the table and make the promise of spring fill the house.

So, I'll leave the barn now. I'll wash up and go inside. I'll take a tumbler and pour a couple of fingers of whiskey, and just like Ralph always did, I'll compliment the parsnips. 'Mighty fine parsnips, Rosemary.'

And if she smiles and if Sarah smiles, the winter chill will leave the house and the season will turn before our eyes. I have no idea how many hay cuttings we'll have this year, I haven't been around here long enough to know things like that yet, but just in case, I'm gearing myself up for three.

The
Woman
in
the
Glass
Booth

TO YOUNG BEN PRICE, who stood at the check-out counter on the main floor of the Towlesport Bookshop, his employer, Miss Currier was monumental as she paced behind the glass walls of her office up on the balcony above the main floor. When she approached the thermo-pane, he could see her underwear through her thin white dress. She was almost twenty years older than he was and her legs were too large. 'Venus under glass' is what Isaac Weed, the paperback clerk, called her. Betty Hamstern, who worked part-time, called Miss Currier their 'Mother Aphrodite.' But, to her salesmanager, Miss Currier was like a massive, white cumulus cloud. He enjoyed the sight of her up in her office. When she cooled herself in front of the air-conditioner, her dress came alive, flopping wildly, and Ben gazed upwards amazed not by her beauty, but by her stature, for Miss Currier was not a physically beautiful woman and did not pretend to be.

One morning Ben got to work early and found her kneeling on the floor in the art corner. A large volume of Greek antiquities was open at her knees. The book's paper was glossy and smooth like the inside of a large shell. She held both hands in front of her, slightly raised, palms upwards. In the left was a slim, cream colored volume from which she was reading aloud,

> "He knows he's very old now, sees it, feels it.
> Yet it seems he was young just yesterday.
> The time's gone by so quickly, gone by so quickly. . . ."

She looked up at Ben. 'Good morning.'

He greeted her and began to straighten books in the nature section, listening to the soft murmer of her reading.

A short while later the others arrived. Betty Hamstern made the coffee and Isaac Weed swept the shipping room. Then, they joined Miss Currier, who was still reading, but silently now, sitting in a chair. They all held white styrofoam cups and stood together watching her. She seemed at peace, alone and deeply absorbed. Finally, Betty Hamstern broke the silence.

'We're all here, Emily,' she said. 'Do you want coffee?'

Miss Currier looked at them. 'Well, hello all. I've been here for hours. What fun this new Cavafy translation is. It came from the wholesaler yesterday. I've ordered fifty more.' She closed the book and used it to beckon them closer. 'Come here. All of you. Ben, you show them that picture.' She pointed to the large book on Greece lying open on the floor. 'Now, look at that terracotta. It's third century, B.C., called "The Birth of Aphrodite." Notice how the statue's left hand is broken. I want you all to guess what our Aphrodite was holding in her hand. What?' Without giving them a chance to respond, she said, 'I say she was reading. Certainly not Cavafy. He's far too late. But reading something. Virgil's *Bucolia* maybe. That's about right. Look how natural it would be for her to be holding a book in her hand.'

Miss Currier kneeled on the carpeting once again and held the Cavafy in imitation of the terracotta in the book.

Isaac Weed looked at her shrewdly over the rim of his steaming coffee cup. 'That's not bad, Miss Currier,' he said.

'She could be looking into a mirror,' said Betty Hamstern.

'She's holding a frog,' said Isaac, giggling.

'She's supposed to be holding a cupid,' said Ben. 'At least, that's what I read somewhere, I think.' He flapped the large book closed. 'Anyway, in this town we'd sell frogs or mirrors or cupids faster than fifty books of poetry. Miss Currier, I say fifty's too many. We might sell five at the most. I can almost name you the customers. Mrs. Fenn, for one.'

As if to shield herself from his criticism, she clutched her breasts and rocked from side to side. 'Oh! You're all so wonderfully brutal. It's such a privilege to have a staff like you three. So many others wouldn't care. But, Ben. My dear, doesn't it amount to the same thing? Mirrors, frogs, cupids and poetry? Doesn't it now? They are all glandular. Are they not?'

'I still say five copies,' said Ben.

Miss Currier didn't hear him. 'Just imagine another shop in Towlesport where there is serious talk of love and poetry at eight-thirty in the morning! Imagine that!' She closed her eyes and smiled, safe and confident of her dominance. 'I know you'll do your best with them. All of you.'

They finished their coffee and opened the doors to the shop.

Betty Hamstern, who was six-feet-two and who piled her hair up adding another four or five inches of illusive height, left her station. 'Well,' she said to Ben Price, 'I guess you've been chosen.'

'What are you talking about?' asked Ben.

'She's been wanting a bright young thing,' said Betty. 'And now she's got you.' Betty started to walk away.

'So what?'

'Just try not to screw it, that's all,' she said. 'We'll all be miserable if you do. Just keep her happy.'

Betty Hamstern's forearms were long enough to carry four wide silver bracelets and each ear could easily take yet a third pierce. As it was, she wore a gold loop in the front of each lobe and a diamond stud after. She was a pretty woman, and when she stood next to Ben, her breasts met his shoulder. She enlarged them sometimes with funnels made of soft foam which did not have quite the same resilience as flesh. Now, she let one of them nudge his shoulder, and it reminded him of a plastic food container and of cole slaw. He knew the contact was not accidental, which flattered him. Betty Hamstern was constantly nudging him like that, standing close to him when they talked. He could smell her lipstick.

From the beginning, Ben wished that Miss Currier had chosen Isaac or even Betty. At times he was able to impress her–a sale of paperback cookbooks in the front window reduced some old inventory at Thanksgiving–but he could not sustain himself. He could not anticipate her wishes nor do her thinking for her. She called him up to her glass-walled office and kept him there over the most trivial matters. They went off on buying trips together. Without embarrassment, Miss Currier began to dote on him and to praise his work to such a degree that it became obvious to the staff as well as to a few regular customers that she was in love.

Ben confided in Betty Hamstern. 'Now, she wants me to go to the jobber with her,' he said. 'To pick Christmas titles. I swear, Betty, I'm not getting my work done. I dream about her.'

Betty was standing close to him. He felt the heat of her body. 'She wants you along,' she said, her breath burning his ear. 'That's what she wants. Woman are selfish.' Then Betty stepped back. 'It's just that she's so obvious about it. She's so damn obvious she makes me sick.'

Though Ben's complaint gravitated, in some warped form, to Miss Currier, she never spoke to him about it. She was willing to let him say anything about her, to make any complaint, and she refused to call him down for what he said. Her affection was pure, and she did not care if she seemed ridiculous to her staff or to the regular customers who noticed the attention she gave him. The emotion Emily Currier felt was the deepest and the most fragile and painful one she had felt for anyone in years. She was quite aware of her age, yet she thrilled at the quickened beat of her heart whenever she thought of him and did not resist it when she felt herself suddenly pliable and soft in his presence. It had been so long since she had felt that giddy, glowing, cloud-ground sensation that she could only resort to melodrama and the saccharin in order to express that which was a true and, at times, a terrifying feeling.

Ben lived alone in a small apartment a mile or so from the bookshop on Sleeper Street. He had no car. When Miss Currier offered to drive him home, he seldom refused. Once, as he was letting himself out of her car, she reached across the seat in the dark and touched his shoulder. 'Oh, Ben!'

When he saw how worn and tired her face was then, he pressed her hand. 'Good night, Emily,' he said. 'Thank you.'

Miss Currier sat outside his apartment house and waited until he disappeared inside. Touching him caused a bitterness to rise in her throat. 'I don't care,' she said, pounding on the steering wheel. 'I don't care, I don't care.' When she was able to see clearly enough to drive, she blew her nose and tooted the horn, good night.

Sales were off at Christmas. Betty Hamstern blamed it on Emily and Ben. They were never there. Usually, people don't steal books, but that season an entire set of Chekhov bound in three quarter morocco walked out of the store. Emily said they would recoup the loss in the spring.

At inventory time, in February, Ben fell off a ladder and sprained his back. He refused to stay home though the pain was so severe that he could not bend over. Then, he slipped on the ice behind the shop and could not get up. Emily was so thoroughly alarmed that her panic infected him. When she took him for x-rays at the hospital on Moulton Road, both of them were limping and pale.

Nothing was cracked nor slipped, and the doctor prescribed a pain pill which reduced his discomfort to an area the size of a saucer in his lower back. He was told to stay off his feet for a week and Emily made him promise to stay off of them for two. 'You will do as I say, young man,' she said. 'You are too valuable to me.'

During his convalescence she became ill herself–the way some males do when they agonize in sympathetic pain during their wives' child-bearing. It was an awkward empathy, to be sure, but she could not help herself from limping and began to need a cane. Then, her wrists swelled, and her cheeks and neck became so enlarged that her jaw line almost completely disappeared. She could not see clearly and wore dark glasses. The jeweler cut off her rings.

She brought him a spider plant. 'Oh, I don't matter,' she said. 'I'll be fine. How are *you*? I want to know how you are.'

'I was out shoveling the walk before,' he said. 'Better, I think. If I take my pills, Emily, it feels like a hot rod burning right here.' He touched the base of his back. 'In the morning, it's worse.'

She grimaced and turned away, imagining his early morning pain, and had to sit down. She found it difficult to breathe in the small, hot room. 'I told you. How many times? You must stay off your feet. And the cold. That's the worst thing you can do for it.' She went to the thermostat and turned up the heat. 'Should I stand guard over you? Ben, how can I keep you in bed? Do I have to move in?'

She didn't realize what she had said until it was too late. 'I mean . . . of course, the world doesn't just stop because you have a sore back.' She sat down, letting her cane fall.

'Maybe you should be in bed, too,' he said. 'You don't look well.'

'I'm not. Look at me.' She removed her dark glasses. 'It's not only my ankles and arms. My clothes are ugly and tight on me. Just look." She parted the front of her blouse to show him the extreme top of her bosom.

Something had happened over the past few months, and he now looked at her, not at her unsightly swelling–that would vanish–but at her. He could see inside of her. It was amazing. Just for a moment, he could actually see all the way inside, and what he saw he was powerless to describe. It was completely amazing, and he was not afraid. What's more, it lasted. They gazed at one another for minutes, it seemed, searching within one another. The only reason he tore his eyes away from hers was because she spoke–her sincere, unrefutable declaration of love made him look away, too confused to reply.

'Don't say anything,' she said, touching his cheek. 'There's plenty of time for that.' He took her hand. They had not held hands before now and he was surprised by how large hers were and how strong. He wanted to tell her that she was beautiful and that he adored her. He wanted to feel her soft body through her dress. 'I'm glad you came,' he said.

Her mouth was warm and soft on his. She breathed on his neck and whispered it to him again and he nodded against her cheek and repeated the phrase after her. 'I do. Yes, I do you too.'

When he looked at her again, she had let her eyes drop to his chest. And he looked away from her as well. He wanted to hold her. He had not felt as full, as vulnerable before in his life. He knew his smile looked pained, and he knew that he could not go to her just now, not yet, not in the way in which he now yearned to. Not now, not with a rod of pain in his back.

More than a week later, Ben was back at the bookshop. Miss Currier had not come in yet and Isaac was putting in a window display. Betty Hamstern took Ben by the arm and led him, straight away, to the shipping room. It was barely light outside and the street was empty. 'At least you've come back,' she said. 'Maybe Emily will be in too.' She released his arm, but stood close. 'It hasn't been easy, you know. I've been sick, too.' She leaned down and whispered in his ear. 'I want you to come to my house after work. I'll give you a drink.'

By nine, Miss Currier had not arrived. She did not come in at all that day. He telephoned and left a message with the cleaning woman. After work, Betty took him to her house. They sat in her living room in front of a gas fire. He knew Betty had been sick, more seriosuly ill than either he or Emily had been. The shop had been without Betty for almost as long as it had been without him. 'Do you really want to know what it was?' she asked. 'It was my breasts. They cut off both my breasts. I'm not ashamed to tell you.' She stood up and raised her drink to her blouse front. 'Both of them are gone.'

'Betty, I'm terribly sorry.'

'Completely gone. It was damn depressing.' She swallowed her drink. Her height was accentuated by the low ceilings. She made another drink and turned to face him. 'Tell me. Honestly. Do I seem less attractive?' She was beside him, looming above him. Her ear rings flashed in the fire light. 'At least you have to admit I'm one hell of a more handsome woman than Emily Currier, even now. You have to admit that. Poor old cow eyes. Ha, our Mother Aphrodite.'

With ease, she could have strangled Ben Price one-handed. 'Yes,' said Ben, 'You're just as attractive, Betty.'

'What about old cow eyes. What's the rest of her like. Flaps and flab. That's what I'll bet.'

He turned away and looked into the fire.

Betty gestured with her thumb at the ceiling. 'Tell me what she's like up there? In the sack. Is she good there?'

Ben was silent.

'Oh, I see, Mr. Lover Boy's not talking. Never kiss and tell. Is that it?'

'You shouldn't say those things,' he said. 'You shouldn't question things like that. It isn't good for you. It makes you bitter.' He looked at her shoes. Quietly, he said, 'Don't be bitter Of course, I think you're pretty. I have always thought that.'

'Me? Are you crazy? I'll never be bitter. I'm happy. I'm God damn happy. That's what. Even if I wasn't, I'd never carry on like she does. At least, I'd keep it a secret.' She had begun to stagger slightly and had to sit down. 'Let me tell you something, Bennie Boy. And it's none of my business. If . . .I'd be damned embarrassed chasing after you the way she did. It's repulsive. If I ever have a boyfriend, no one, and I mean no one, will know about it. Especially not you people at the bookshop. You won't catch me necking in the shipping room. Not ever. I can promise you that.' As she spoke, her hands hovered absently at her chest. She patted the cloth of her blouse. Then, she stood up and drew herself to her full height. 'Also, I can have anyone I want, any time I want. Inspite of this.' She steadied herself by hanging onto the back of a chair. 'There are ways. Believe you me. Ways. In case you haven't heard. A woman can compensate.'

For the first time in days, the hot rod in the small of his back returned.

'You can fool them too, if you have to. Even in bed. Breasts aren't everything. What do you see in her anyway?'

'You mean in Emily?' he asked. 'And not in you? Is that it?'

'Let me give you more to drink. I want to know about her. I want more.'

As she handed him a full glass, he looked up at her and smiled. He smelled a faint trace of moth balls in her blue wool skirt and bath soap. 'I don't know if I can tell you, exactly,' he said.

'Well, I think it's sick, if you really want to know. You should take a look at her sometime, take a real close look.'

'I think I have,' he said.

'Like hell.'

'I better go.'

'Finish your drink.' she was towering over him again. 'I don't see how you can bring yourself. I can't see it. Not you two. Not ever.'

He lurched for the door.

The cold air was an enormous relief. 'You look at her sometime,' he said walking down the sidewalk. 'You look for yourself.' He had gone half a block before he realized that Betty had not driven him home as she had offered so that now he had more than twice the usual distance to walk. He found his knit hat in his coat pocket and pulled it down over his ears against the bitter wind coming off the river. His back wasn't bothering him that much, though he limped slightly. In what seemed like no time at all, he was fumbling for the keys to his apartment against the incessant ringing of his telephone. It was Emily.

Nowadays, when Ben Price looks up at her from his station on the main floor, she is smiling at him–not down but *at* him–through the thermo-pane windows in her office. She is no longer an enormous cumulus cloud. She is no longer Venus Under Glass. Nor is she Mother Aphrodite kneeling before a book which has brittle, shell-like paper.

The
New
Wing

IN TOWLESPORT, the bus let him off at Lunt's Drug. He went inside to telephone. It was September and the incongruous smells of magazines, pills and shampoo which was circulated by the store's forced air heating made his face sting. Tom Snow was relieved there was no one in the store that he knew. He looked tired, like a working stiff, puffy and red-eyed. He and his wife had argued, and Snow had left. He had been away for three full weeks. Now, he was back again and no one answered the telephone at home.

As he walked from Lunt's to his house, he noticed that all around him the season had changed. Leaves were falling on the houses and here was the bitter smell of the sea in the air. As if he were uncertain of his right to be there at all, he nodded to the people he passed on the sidewalk. He asked the small tartish girl who waited tables at Cottle's Pizza how business was, and she gave him a mean look and crossed the street. 'I must look odd,' he said aloud as he turned around to watch the waitress walk. Her hips rolled with each step and then twitched. He was amazed that girls, women, wore such revealing clothes these days, especially in front. One minute they were wearing long skirts and the next they were pouring themselves into shorts and pants, threatening to chew out the seams. He wondered again where he had been, just as he wondered where the summer had gone.

The hot flash of lust for the tartish girl had not left him when he turned down his own street. He waved blindly to a neighbor who was raking his sidewalk. Though they lived two doors apart, Snow knew little more about Daniel Fenn than his name. The Fenns had a nice looking house from the outside, equally as old and as well restored as his own.

His wife's car was not in the garage and the doors were locked. He found no key in their secret place under the cedar planter by the back door. He walked full circle around the house. The rooms looked barren. Usually, if Lauri was staying out after dark, she left the light on in the front hall.

Using a steel stake which supported the withering tomato plants, he broke the latch on the bulkhead which led down cellar. As he fumbled his way to the back stairs, he was surprised that he didn't bump into anything. He pulled the light cord over the stairs. It had no bulb in it. Upstairs, he found the furniture, the rugs and all of her clothing had disappeared. The shock struck him like a severe blow to the chest over the heart and he had to sit down on the floor in the dining room. There was no need to call the police. Hurt and angry now, he searched the house room by room. She had left him with a chair and a table in the living room and a card table and a low stool in the kitchen and a few pots and pans and his slide projector.

At least she hadn't taken all the liquor. With a drink in one hand and a stick of firewood in the other, he wandered through the empty house again and again. 'Lauri?' he called to her quietly, tempting her as in hide-and-seek. 'Lauri Snow? I'm coming to get you. I know you're here somewhere.' The panic built in him. 'Lauri, God damn you, come out!' He pounded the stick of firewood on the bare floor of the bedroom. He yelled into the empty linen closet. 'You bitch! For God's sake, stop this game and come out of there.' For the better part of an hour, he called after her. 'It's me, Honey,' he said, sitting on the rim of the bath tub, holding his head in his hands. 'It's old Tom. Don't be afraid. Please, come to me.'

He found no trace of her–not a nylon, not a bobbie pin, not a tube of cream. She was gone. He now understood that as an undeniable fact. The echo of his feet on the rugless floors unsettled him, increasing the alarming fact of her absence.

It was nearly midnight when he built a fire in the living room and went to sleep on his coat. The following morning he called his office and said he was going to stay home a few days. In the morning light, the house seemed emptier still. He telephoned his friends, but stopped calling when he realized how foolish he seemed to them, searching for his wife as one looks for a lost animal.

She had left him some food. Somehow eating helped. Also, he was amazed by how much time it took to fend for himself–to cook and wash the dishes, to sweep and to take care of the trash. In the afternoon, he called the furniture store and ordered a foam mattress, which he laid in front of the fireplace.

He brought in a supply of firewood which he piled on the living room floor. In the shed, he had stacked two cords of swamp maple, plus some locust and iron wood. The locust was ant ridden. He grew tired of stepping on the large black ants and decided to let them wander at will. He got down on his hands and knees and yelled at a party of ten making its way towards the kitchen. 'You have a reprieve!' he yelled. 'I give you an extension on your life! Go now and remake your nest in my floorboards and cupboards.'

As the days passed, though he shunned his friends and neglected his work, he did not allow himself to become diminished by the lack of clutter and by the absence of her low persistent voice in the barren house. At times, he actually felt his spirit expanding, taking up the space where her belongings had once been. It was as if a pressure had been removed from him, and he talked to himself aloud without embarrassment.

One night after hash and canned tomatoes, he set his after-dinner drink on the table in the living room and set up the screen and slide projector. He had a desire to see his wife again. It had been more than three weeks and he could no longer visualize her clearly. In the cabinet in the den, he found a carousel tray which he assumed held a picture of her.

He set the screen close to his chair.

The first slide, margined in the black of the screen, was a picture of the house he had taken from the driveway. It was reduced to the size of a piece of ordinary writing paper. 'Shrunk,' he said aloud, remembering an earlier time when he had actually believed the house had suddenly become too small for them. He admired his house for a time and, before switching slides, decided that, yes, it's really a lovely house. 'It was lovely even before I built the new wing–"Lauri's New Wing", he said. He clicked to the next slide which was the mid-section of a door, a plain pine door with a peculiar latch from which a sign was hanging. He recognized the sign as being the one she had hurriedly scrawled and hung outside their wedding chamber in Grand Exuma. He used it, now and again, when he slept alone in the guest room, away from, her, after a quarrel.

Next on the screen was 'Lauri's Lawn.' He had hired a landscaper to roll it out as a surprise on their third anniversary. Her 'Venus Shell' came next, the swimming pool. That was for their fifth.

As he reached for his drink, his hand bumped the reverse button. The circular tray began to click methodically backwards. He stopped it at the 'Do Not Disturb' sign. It was a Saturday morning that past spring. He had spent the night in the guest room and slept late. A few minutes before ten o'clock, she flung the door open without knocking. She wore a bright scarf made from silk and an off-white dress he had never seen before. Towering above him, she tore the sign in half and tossed the pieces onto the bed. 'So, you're still here?' she asked.

He was about to reply when he noticed two people in coats standing behind her in the hall. He pulled his covers up to his chin. 'Who are they?'

Without replying, she turned to the couple. 'It's quite all right,' she said. 'This would be your room. I want you to see the bath.'

An older woman with a deeply lined and sympathetic face, followed by a short man with a thin mustache, filed through the room into the bath. Tom nodded in response to the small man's brief smile.

His wife's voice reverberated in the shower stall. 'Two men lived here before us. They put in the bidet. We never use it, except sometimes to soak plants.'

He shaved and dressed. After the couple had gone, he went outside to find her. She was cutting back the climbing roses on the deck off the dining room.

'Lauri? I think we should talk about this.'

'What's there to talk about. I need help. She'll cook and keep the place clean. The husband can do your yard work.'

'But I like to do the yard work.'

'Of course, the house is too small the way it is. I'm pinched living here, Thomas. We need more space.' she said. 'I want a new wing.'

Alone now, in the darkened room, Snow clicked the slides ahead–ashamed. He had acquiesced. He hadn't even faked a protest. 'Lauri's Lawn' flashed by. 'The Venus Shell.' He drained his glass.

Lauri had one flaw, a line of dark hair on her upper lip. Contrasted with her extraordinary good looks, the faint mustache and her low voice left him, time and time again, as helpless as if he were chained to her, to her beauty and to her strength.

It had gotten dark outside and he went around downstairs turning on what lights there were–hall, half-bath, dining room overhead, the floods in the ceiling in the sun room, stairs, wet bar. While he was there, he made another drink. It seemed like years had passed, not months. It had taken him just under five months to build the addition, 'Lauri's New Wing.'

The next slide on the screen held great interest for Snow. It was a slab of concrete which abutted the house. At the far end, splattered with cement, there he stood as erect and as proud as a sentry. How much younger he looked, those few months ago. He radiated vitality. Snow smiled as he recalled the events which led up to that final, tumultuous excitement he felt the day the footings and the slab for the addition were poured.

It began on the morning Lauri interviewed the older couple–the old cook and gardener. He had climbed up the side of the house on a ladder to take off the storm windows and he realized that he felt like an awkward giant. The house seemed to have shrunk, unaccountably, shrunk by a third. Until that moment, he had never suspected the house was too small for her. Well, if it's too small, he decided, I'll do something about it. He stored the storm windows in the shed and called Henry Farnham, a friend and real estate agent, who had begun and abandoned a career in architecture. 'Let me take you to Cottle's Pizza for lunch,' Snow said over the telephone. 'I've got an architectural commission for you. We're going to put a wing on the house. We both decided on it this morning.'

They sat across from one another at one of the round tables which had been painted by a local craftsman to stimulate a pepperoni and mushroom pizza. 'Are you sure you want to add on?' Farnham asked, both his elbows resting on the imitation pizza. 'I'm about to list a nice cape on Plum Street. You can have first look.'

Snow's hands were folded on top of a painted mushroom. 'We like it where we are, Henry. Lauri thinks the house is too small.'

'Small? Your place is a bleeding castle. What does she want?'

'Well, she's talking live-ins–an older couple. But, there's not enough room. We'd all have to share the bath.'

Though it was impossible, Snow thought he actually saw a light bulb flashing a few inches above Henry Farnham's green tyrolean hat.

Farnham slapped the table. His hand landed on a barren expanse of tomato sauce and whey colored cheese. 'Ah, ha! I've got it now! So, she's talking live-ins.'

'I think I know what you're thinking, Henry. Well, stop it. They're an older couple–retired.' Snow looked at the table and pulled a napkin from the dispenser to wipe his hands. Afterwards, he kept them in his lap. 'He'd help with the yard work and she'd do the cooking and cleaning. It's not what you think. Everything's fine with us. The Vo-Tech instructor is part of the past. She hasn't time to do everything herself.'

'That's how far you know, old buddy.' Farnham was smiling to himself the way he did after he made a sale and the buyers had gone away.

Snow leaned toward him, resisting the impulse to put his hands on the table. 'Why, Henry, do you know something about her that I don't?' He had a freezing sensation in his gut, which was followed by an embarrasing grumble. Suddenly, he had a burning need for the bathroom.

The graffiti on a section of the gray wall unsettled him. Someone offering a variety of sexual services had left a telephone number, and Snow read it as his own listing. He read it again after he had quieted down and saw that the last two numbers were transposed and the listening was not his after all. But, somehow, he couldn't let it drop.

'You're crazy,' Farnham told him, his mouth full. 'I don't know anything about it. Tommy, I'd tell you if I did.'

'Forgive me,' said Snow, knowing Henry Farnham would do nothing of the kind.

In the end, Farnham sketched a set of plans and charged a quarter of what it would have cost Snow elsewhere. In fact, the savings on that count got him to calculating. He decided to contract the job himself with the help of his neighbor, Salvatore Bianchini, who had built by his own count twenty-five houses in Essex county alone.

'It's jackass work, Tommy,' said Bianchini. 'Jackass work. If you want to do your own jackass work, that's fine by me. I'll make sure your walls go up straight and the roof stays on, but remember this. I'm the boss on this job. You're working for me.'

On the day Henry Farnham passed over the plans, Snow called Bianchini. While the short, huge gutted Italian absorbed himself in them, Snow went outside. It was drizzling and the wind had begun to kick up from the north east. He filled his lungs with the warm smell of the sea. Looking at the house through the weather, he could visualize 'Lauri's New Wing'.

'Oh, Lauri,' he said aloud. 'Do you know the thrill of this? It's more tremendous than the lawn or the pool.' As if in response, a rolling clap of thunder sounded and the sky opened, releasing streams of spring rain. 'I'll build it with my own back,' he yelled. 'With my own hands and brains.' He raised his voice against the sound of falling water and the wind. 'How proud you'll be!' he sang into the core of the storm. 'How proud.' Intoxicated by his own excitement and oblivious to the weather, he stood in the corner of his yard and visualized the new wing. Charged now with massive emotion, he raced across the wet lawn and burst into the kitchen. 'When can we start? When, Sal? When can we?' He was drenched and breathless and sounded like an unrestrainable child.

Bianchini, who had found a beer in the refrigerator, looked up from the plans and shook his head. 'As soon as I get the mud. You dig the footings and make the forms. Make them deep.' He gave his instructions with his hands. 'Allow for a two foot footing and a six inch slab.' He rolled up the plans. 'I'll check it before we pour. Don't catch cold.' He drained his beer and put on his cap. Thunder sounded again. Bianchini raised his collar and disappeared into the ribbons of falling rain.

When the cement truck came, Snow was in Boston. It left two deep ruts in the lawn. Out back he found Bianchini, a cement covered dwarf, on his hands and knees finishing off the slab with a long straight-edge. He swore at Snow. 'Where the living hell have you been? Pushing paper when I need you the most.'

'I'll change and be right out.'

'No time. Strip.'

Snow removed his street shoes, suit and coat and necktie.

Bianchini yanked the straight-edge out of his hands. 'You'll ruin those pants. I ain't modest.'

He kept on his underwear and his socks.

It was sunset when they finished. Tom's knees were caked with dried cement. 'Look at it,' he said. 'Just look! I want a picture of this.'

'Merciful Lord.'

Snow, posed with the straight-edge at his side, looked alert and vigorous. Bianchini, wearing his cap backwards, took the picture. Then Tom got them beers and took one of Salvatore sitting on the running board of his truck.

Now, peering intently at the slide on the screen, the freshly poured slab seem to Snow to almost quiver.

Throughout the construction, he had recorded such moments. Slide by slide, he watched the addition take shape once again. Studs, siding, Anderson windows, cedar clapboards, shingle roof, staircase, wallboard, and finally the copper cupolas over the bedroom windows pounded and shaped by the roofer, Michael Blue.

He clicked back to the tapers.

Both he and Lauri were home when the tapers arrived to tack up the wallboard. They drank a glass of wine and watched the three French-Canadians in their white coveralls. Each had a bright red bandana tied around his neck. They cleared the scrap from the floor and strapped on aluminium stilts. Conducting themselves with exemplary ease in the pure white room, like a variety of enormous crane, they concealed nailheads and seams with tape, which they further covered with wall compound.

Tom had snapped one of them as he smiled down at Lauri. Now as he examined the slide, he noticed that the taper's expression was frank and lustful. She had allowed the taper to look at her like that, he realized, she had invited him to look at her like that.

'I hope it's going to be large enough,' she had said. Her forehead came just to the taper's knee.

'It's too late now if it isn't.'

'Did I tell you that Henry Farnham asked me for lunch today? I told him I couldn't. I mean, he's your friend.'

'He can be yours too, if you want.'

'We went to Wolfe's Tavern after work. He wants me to study for the real estate test. God, Thomas, he's so damn funny. He actually thinks I can sell real estate.'

'He should know. Do you want to try?'

'You know, I almost think I would. But, it scares me. I mean, it's difficult to sell. To get out there and push something. I don't think I could.'

'Henry will help. I'm sure of that.'

Lauri took the test and passed easily. At the time, Snow thought it was because of his wife's native ability with mathematics.

As well as photographing the progress of the construction, Snow had taken pictures of almost every workman–a sort of rogue's gallery of moonlighting union men and retired laborers whom Bianchini had rounded up God knows where–

Young Otto Cutting, carpenter and self-avowed ladies' man,

Crab, the electrician, who worked out of his basement,

Lionel Clark, imported tiles,

Happy the Plumber, a compulsive gambler who once lost 'three hundred grand' on a bender,

Walt 'Fingers' Corey, Anderson windows and skylights.

When the next slide appeared, Snow burst out laughing. 'There's Bianchini the day we poured the slab. Jesus, that was some job, hey Sal? Bianchini was sitting on the running board of his truck with a beer, scowling at the camera.

Snow advanced the carousel tray–

Lee Stone, heating,

John Fuentes and Carlos Salte, painters—exterior and interior,

Michael Blue, the roofer, copper and tin.

Snow leaned back in his chair. Just to see Blue up there on the roof, molding the copper domes which capped the two picture windows over the bedroom, saddened him. As a present, Bianchini had given him that copper weathervane on the left dome to celebrate finishing the job. It was a silhouette of a man chasing his hat.

Snow left the picture on the screen and went to the bar. Sure. It wasn't fantastic living with her. He knew that. Still, it wasn't that bad. His love may have been too benign and hers too passionate. Still, they got along without too much pain or bitterness or too much deceit–if you didn't count her passionate episodes, the Vo-Tech instructor from Hampton Falls the previous winter and, more recently, her gynocologist. At the time, he hardly felt either of them. All he asked was to know who it was. It was less difficult, somehow, if he knew who and if he didn't have to suspect every man who put his eyes on her. While Lauri and her doctor were carrying on and on, he took the early bus to Boston and had his coffee and a dry roll at the office. Usually, her lovers clouded their lives for two or three months, at the most, before they left as silently, and as faceless, as they had come. He didn't believe she was truly unfaithful, not deeply unfaithful. He accepted her passionate and wandering nature and called it 'Lauri's Search'. After all, he was no expert in landscape gardening and certainly no expert in women's matters. When she wanted the yard landscaped, she found a Vo-Tech man. When she lost the child, she found her doctor. Sure. Maybe she got too close to them, but that was her nature. She never loved them and she came away from them a stronger person, she claimed. After all, how could a woman as fine as Lauri love a Vocational Technology Instructor or a Gynocologist or, for that matter a Real Estate Agent?

He made his drink and approached the living room. His walk had a peculiar lurching motion to it, as if he were an unsteady passenger aboard a ship in a storm. He found his chair and sat down. The sight of the roofer on the screen had blurred. He blinked trying to focus. The slide showed Michael Blue, a silhouette against the horizon, gazing out over the roof lines, over the trees onto the sea. The simple serenity of the roofer's gaze relaxed him. It allowed Snow to see those past months with clarity. With ease he could now ask himself who her latest lover was. Who it was she hadn't told him about, who had made them fight, who had sent him away to Boston for three full weeks, who she was living with now and where he could find her. And with equal, almost astonishing, ease, he heard the answer as clearly as if Lauri had told him herself. He waited for his breath to leave him, to be struck in the chest. 'Henry Farnham,' he said, softly, with his hand over his mouth. 'Well, well, old Henry.' He exhaled. 'But it doesn't matter. It doesn't matter any more.'

The whirring projector annoyed him now. He sat for a time in the dark room. His breathing seemed to be amplified in the emptiness. He was thoroughly aware now that he was alone, entirely alone, that the carousel held no slide of his wife.

The only photograph he had was one which he carried in his wallet. Using the light from the overhead in the dining room, he opened his wallet and laid it down. He sat cross legged on the bare floor and gazed at her. She was maneuvering a small sailboat close to shore. The yellow hull, the turquoise water and the darker blue sky were a cheerful contrast to the striped sail and to her gaily colored scarf. She was smiling the way she used to smile at him.

'Hey, Lauri,' he said, waving at her. 'You're wearing that scarf. Look. You're wearing the ear rings I bought for you at the export shop.' The memories which welled and flooded through him, carried him forward as if he were riding a wave. On and on he talked to the photograph. It was sentiment and liquor talking. He knew it. But he had to say goodbye to her and to that part of his life. It was time for that. He had to bring her back full blown in order to let her go, to let that part of him be free. The unsettling feeling of an insect on his skin startled him. He raised his hand, instinctively, to swat the large carpenter ant crawling up his arm. Instead, he shook it off onto the floor. What was he going to remake himself into now? The ants were weeks ahead of him. Something. He'd do something.

He got up from the floor and began to wander. The fire was low and he didn't bother to add more wood.

He lay down on his foam mattress and slept fitfully at first. Later, he dreamed. And, in his dream, all of them, every one of her lovers paraded in front of him, but they were not laughing. No, not even Henry Farnham was laughing at him. His head filled with voices. They were like black metallic leaves screaming in a hot wind. He dreamed of water. And the warmth of his tears on his cheeks awoke him. 'Lauri's gone,' he said. He whispered the fact again and again into the dark, empty living room. He rolled over onto his side to face the dying fire. Her spirit left him then. He could actually feel the finality of the loss, and the relief. As he fell asleep, the rooms expanded further still. He changed positions. Lying on his back, he received both the house as it enlarged around him and the onslaught of emptiness.

Daniel
Fenn,
Unhobbled
and
Unhinged

MY NAME IS DANIEL FENN. I live in Towlesport, a coastal town in Massachusetts on the Merrimac River, and the commuter bus from Boston always lets me off at the end of my street a few minutes before six o'clock. It is a five minute walk down Cottle's Lane to my front door.

On the bus, I usually sit next to my friend Nelson Greenleaf who lives up my street. While crossing the Mystic River Bridge, we talk and share the evening paper. For the last few minutes of the ride, between Boxford and Towlesport, I fall asleep. One evening, as we arrived, I found myself thinking about my secretary. Earlier in the day, she had said, casually, that now that fall was here it was time to break off old love affairs to begin new ones. I laughed. Her remark sounded odd, coming as it did from nowhere, without provocation. But, the more I considered it, the truer it became, as if she had planted the idea in my mind.

Briefly, I thought she might be asking or testing me, but her eyes did not swerve. Besides, I neither had a lover to break-up with nor was I looking for one. My wife did not make me unhappy and I considered myself throughly bound, chained, tied, hobbled and lucky. I had been married to Michelle for almost eight years at the time and was resigned to riding back and forth to Boston each weekday, reading the paper on the way in and the paper on the way out, napping between Boxford and Towlesport. What repetition and dullness I felt was not abhorrent. Long ago I decided that the small moments in one's life, the series of small challenges and disappointments, are enough. That was over five months ago. My primary regret, a vain one which remains, is that my nose is too long and thin and my eyes are too close together, as if my head was caught in a vice and pulled and pinched at birth.

As usual, the commuter bus discharged us at the top of Cottle's Lane. One passenger back-tracked a few hundred feet and crossed the Rowley Turnpike. Three went into Lunt's Drug to stand in line at the pay phone. Nelson and I walked down Cottle's Lane together.

The Greenleaf's house came first. 'It's Friday, Dan,' he said. 'Stop for a while.'

Knowing me, I probably pulled my nose before I accepted. While Nelson built a fire, I sat on the couch holding my glass. 'Wheew!' I said. 'You make a drink.'

A few minutes later, Helen Bryant-Greenleaf's younger sister, a girl of eighteen or so, came running downstairs. Her long dark hair was still wet from her bath. When she sat next to me on the couch, our hips touched slightly. Normally, I would have moved away, but the contact seemed harmless. I could smell soap–probably it was shampoo, a faint herbal smell–and was amazed that she seemed interested. My office fatigue left me then; the girl and the drink were cheering, especially when I found that I was able to make her laugh. As we talked, I discovered that I could not stop looking at her dark eyes, her long smooth neck, her breasts. And she seemed to like my looking, at least, she gave me no sign that I was rude. She had the habit of leaning quite close when she spoke and her breath on my face was sweet and made me want to close my eyes.

I seldom whistle under any circumstances. But, as I walked home in the dark that night, after a couple of belts of Greenleaf's booze, a short, bright tune, one I had never heard anywhere before, burst from my lips. A northeast wind was up and brought with it fog and the sour brine smell from the clam flats. I lowered my head presenting my song to a dog ripping at a paper sack. The dog cocked its head and snarled before it dragged the sack away out of the street light. Words for the tune would not form in my mind. I let myself whistle, simply whistle, all the way home, where I found my wife, kneeling in the garden with a flashlight, harvesting the last of the green tomatoes before the frosts.

'I was worried,' said Michelle, 'so I came out here. You must have done something right today.' She abused my eyes with the flashlight.

I waved her remark aside without interrupting my song. The tune ran around and around itself, bursting with uncommon gaiety in the living room. I have no words to describe the sensations which were running through me then. I couldn't tell Michelle that a chance meeting with a girl almost twenty years younger than myself had filled me with life again. I couldn't say that even to myself. When she came in from the garden, I embraced her, holding her tighter and longer than she wanted.

'Where have you been? I smell whiskey.'

I told her what had happened, sort of, and how the girl had run downstairs. When I tried to whistle again, I found the tune had left me. I could not repeat it and whistled 'Row, Row, Row Your Boat!' instead, then I stopped whistling.

'At least you're in a good mood for a change,' she said. 'I don't care if you are trite.'

'Yes you do,' I said, as I took her pretty oval face in my hands and kissed her.

On Wednesday morning, the following week, I caught the early bus and stopped at the Ritz for breakfast where the coffee is served in large silver-colored pots and the croissants taste almost as good as those I found once early in the morning in Paris and was never able to find again. Though I'm certain it isn't true, I like to believe that the *New York Times* is delivered to the newsstand in the lobby of the Ritz before it is delivered anywhere else in the city, with the ink still wet. I usually sit at one of the small tables by the window. That particular morning, across the room, I recognized an old shipmate from the Navy. He was eating eggs and breakfast meat with half a dozen men and, from all appearances, had successfully transformed himself from a Lieutenant Junior Grade into a banker. He didn't recognize me. Or, if he did, he made no indication. From behind my newspaper, I realized how little I knew about him. I could no longer remember his name nor his station aboard the aircraft carrier to which we both were assigned. A while later, I looked across the room and he was gone.

On the way to the office at the corner of Dartmouth and Commonwealth, I noticed a woman in levis. She wore her hair in a red cloth and was unloading boxes from a U-Haul van. She was about to disappear inside an apartment building.

Laura Moore is short. Her hair was blonde again. Though she had gained weight, I would recognize that woman anywhere and would cross an eight lane highway to get to her. The last time I saw her was on Fifth Avenue in New York on a Sunday. Michelle and I were visiting friends for the weekend and were on our way out of town. She was with her first husband, an architect whom I never knew very well, and had frosted her hair and styled it formally. Smooth and sprayed, it looked as if she were wearing a chromed war helmet. I pulled over to the curb and called out to her. She wore an elegant dress and her husband had on evening clothes. They both looked ten years older than their mid-twenties, and their extravagant clothing distinguished them in the crowd. 'We're out for some air,' Laura told me. 'We're giving a huge party and the caterers sent us away.' I introduced Laura to Michelle. They shook hands through the window of the station wagon. We talked until a bus honked, then Laura disappeared in the crowd and Michelle and I crossed town and drove north to Towlesport, arriving about one in the morning, just as Laura's party approached its elegant height. The next I heard from her was that she had divorced the architect and was living in Paris learning to paint.

'Laura Windgate,' I now shouted across Commonwealth Avenue. Windgate was her married name. She didn't hear me. 'Laura Moore!'

That stopped her. She turned on the steps and squinted in my direction.

'Hello? I can't see who you are. Come closer.'

Laura's complexion was always smooth and her coloring light. Though her face was rounder, her skin was still pure–as pure as I remembered it fifteen years before, when she was in her late teens and I was in my early twenties and we were lovers for an entire summer at her parent's lake house in the Adirondacks. One of the last things she sent me, along with the letters, was a photograph she had taken of me standing under a birch by the lake. I was smoking a cigarette and wore my Navy uniform and was a good deal trimmer than I am now.

I took the steps two at a time. We kissed and held one another for a moment. She was heavier than I remembered and a good foot shorter than my wife. I felt tall embracing her and she pressed her cheek against my breast bone, as she had done many times before. She was not so heavy that I couldn't lift her off the steps. 'Put me down, you,' she said in just the same way she used to years ago. That made us laugh. She is a splendid woman. Simply splendid. To think, I might very well have married her–if it hadn't been our ages and the Navy and a few other obstacles of adolescence.

Each of us carried a box upstairs. The apartment was fully furnished, including a baby grand piano. She threw a pair of trousers into a closet. 'He's a pianist,' she said. 'We met on the right bank of the Seine–that is the Left. I've known him since we were children. His family, that is.' She left me alone and went down to the street to lock up the van.

While she was gone, I did something I had not done before. I telephoned the office to tell my secretary that I would be in later in the day, if at all.

Laura and I talked and talked. Then, I offered to carry the remaining boxes. Of course, I was stalling, curious to meet her pianist. And Peter Salisbury was waiting for her when we got back from returning the van. He was shorter than Laura, thin, and exceedingly jovial. His fingers were stubby, which did not limit the number of pieces he could play, because of his remarkable span. He relaxed immediately after Laura told him who I was and made us all drinks before lunch. Soon, he became tired of Laura's and my incessant flow of reminescences and began to practice the piano. He was working on Mozart's 'Piano Sonata in B Flat Major' trying, as he explained, for a lyric interpretation. He wanted none of the mechanisms in the piece–the slow repetition of themes, the sudden cadences and so forth–to show. His playing was fluid, but somehow muted. Still, he played extraordinarily well and repeated various sections from the first movement two and three times for us. Now, whenever I hear that particular Mozart sonata, I recall the day I played hookey from the office to be with Laura Moore.

I arranged a dinner for Laura and Peter. The meal came off as a

Fenn dinner usually does. Michelle's elaborate preparation, the hesitant greeting at the door, a paced cocktail hour that always runs too long for Michelle, the burst of energetic conversation as each finishes the first helping and goes back for more, a prolonged dessert, coffee, a brandy in the living room which sends them home full and sleepy, each only half recalling wisps and clots of the conversation. Too soon Michelle and I were left with a house full of dishes and ashtrays and half empty glasses.

As I moved about the room, carrying the remnants of the evening into the kitchen to be washed, I realized that I had hardly spoken to Laura. There had been no words, no topics I cared to share with her in the presence of my wife and Peter Salisbury. The only intimate moment I had with her all evening occurred now. The glass she had used at dinner held a small glowing pool of wine in the bottom. First, I glanced at my wife's back. Then I drained the glass. A shiver of pleasure passed through my body as I swallowed. I let my lips linger on the rim. I didn't feel foolish in the slightest–thrilled, yes, and slightly ashamed. I touched the tines on the dessert fork she had used. A few years before in a museum in Madrid I had done much the same thing and thought of it now. The guard's back was turned I used the moment to reach up and feel the cool marble breast of a stature I had been admiring. Much the same thrill of shame and pleasure had passed through me then. During the evening, when I looked at Laura, she had let me look. She focused her eyes beyond me, as if she were looking at a spot at the back of my skull. From habit, she arched her back to accentuate her breasts. She was always proud of her body and seemed to ask to be admired. About that evening, I remember nothing she said, I remember only the way she lifted her fork and used her napkin and the way she put on her coat, pulling it shut when she left, as if she were closing a curtain upon a dramatic scene.

I carried the plates into the kitchen. Michelle was rinsing the salad bowl. 'She seems very nice. Young, certainly, and quiet. Pretty and nice. I can't believe she's been married before.'

'We had a fine conversation,' I said. 'I don't know what it was about.'

'Does it matter?'

Michelle was waiting to see what I was going to do about Laura, if, in fact, I was going to do anything at all.

'I like her enormously,' I said. 'I always have. Did you?'

'Certainly. I noticed you do.'

About our summer together, I remember best all the places where we made love, especially the one or two nights we drove off the Moore's dock into the black water and swam out to the sailboat. The rest of the summer is fuzzy, yet I'm sure we were not totally preoccupied with sex. We were easy with ourselves and didn't have to prove anything. I suppose that we acted as if it would go on forever. Lying with Laura in the hull of the sailboat was like soaring. Lying with her–we were both wet and naked and young. I cherish that memory as much as I do any that I hold. But it didn't go on forever. The Navy assigned me to an aircraft carrier which was home–ported in Boston. Laura met her architect in New York. I met Michelle a year or so before my hitch in the Navy was up and that was that.

A few days after the dinner party, I called Laura and asked her to meet for lunch. She suggested a place on Newbury street which was not far from the office. I was seated in the restaurant and half way through a martini when she burst–yes, she literally seemed to explode–into the room. She rubbed her hands together, accepting the steamy warmth of the room, took off her scarf and shook out her hair. She waved, ignoring the hostess, and cut across the room to my table. She offered her cheek, flushed and cold. Before she sat down, she did a remarkable, but very Laura-like thing. She looked at me the way she had during supper that night, focusing somewhere at the back of my skull, and reached for the hem of her sweater to pull it off. The gesture was intimate. When her head emerged from the neck of the turned-inside-out sweater, she hesitated, still looking at me, and waited, giving me time to admire her neat, sheer blouse and skirt. 'I got dressed up for you,' she said. 'No one ever asks me out to lunch.'

I ordered a bottle of wine. She had a glass while I drank a

second martini. She ordered pâté before her omlette. I had the snails, which we shared. When I held my fork to her mouth, she took my hand. She closed her eyes to receive the food. We touched again–that is, our fingers touched–when we sopped the juice in the snail dish.

But something was missing. Something was not being said.

'Where's Peter?' I asked.

'Oh, him. Somewhere. A lesson, I think.'

Though I always feel completely at ease with her, spontaneous and affectionate, something was missing.

'I wish you didn't have to go back to work,' she said. 'Let's do this again, when you have more time.' She took my hand and pulled it close to her. I understood the gesture to mean that she didn't think my nose was too long nor that my eyes were set too close together.

Afterwards, we walked down Newbury Street. First I stopped walking, then she did. We looked at one another, and I believe we were about to kiss when a man huddled in a doorway said something obscene. I looked down at him and he pretended he was talking to a group of pigeons. His voice was harsh and foreign. Laura was prepared to ignore the old drunk.

'Will you walk me back to the office?'

'I'd planned on it.'

Yet, we did kiss. I held her face and we kissed–a quick and friendly goodbye–before I watched her walk back to her apartment. Her habit was not to turn and wave when she left someone. Laura never turns and waves. It is a rule of hers. She dismisses the person she has been with and presses ahead, presses onward. I returned to work that afternoon feeling irritable and vaguely unfulfilled.

Throughout the fall and early winter, at least once a week, I went to Laura's apartment for lunch. I have to admit that she is not a particularly good cook, however she is a fine hostess. Our lunches were formal. Usually, Peter ate with us. Laura set the table with elaborate care and wore a long dress. We all seemed so adult at those times, so middle-aged and so prosperous. Also, the grace and formality of our meals together served to inhibit us somewhat. After all, Laura was flanked by two of her lovers. Peter laid claim to her present, and I to a portion, however significant, of her past. I listened politely to any pressing domestic matters, and Peter to our endless chatter–or he excused himself and played the piano. I had no idea that all through that fall and early winter Peter and Laura had been quarreling and had begun to drift apart.

A few weeks before Chistmas, she called me.

'You promised you'd come and see me after work sometime. Why haven't you?'

'I'd like that. Tomorrow? I can drive into town so I won't have to worry about catching the bus.'

'Peter's away,' she said. Her telephone voice was almost sultry, sleepy and deep.

The following evening, when I rang the bell, she opened the door immediately, as if she had been waiting. She wore shorts and a t-shirt which had 'Put Some Fun Between Your Legs' written across the front. Again, she gave me 'her look' as I now called it.

I am not a slow reader, but it seemed to take hours to read the writing on her front. It was odd to be alone with her, too intimate almost. I felt the color rise in my cheeks.

'I've bought a bicycle,' she said. 'The shirt came with it. Do you get it?'

'I think I do.'

The apartment was hot. In the kitchen, she had a pitcher of martinis ready and two glasses set out. 'I almost never drink these. If I get drunk, Daniel, at least you won't have to carry me home.' She handed me a glass and led the way. 'You haven't really seen the apartment. Have you?'

I followed her into her bedroom. 'This is our bed.'

We stood at the edge of what seemed a very large vacant plain. Laura's perfume struck me as being too strong.

Then, she laughed. 'Oh, come on. It's only a bed.'

We sat on the couch in the living room. Her t-shirt distracted me. Finally she said, 'You married men are all so strange. You take everything too seriously. A New York friend of mine was staying here last week while Peter was away. He brought me tons and tons of food. After the first night, his wife called and told him to either come home or to move into a hotel. He didn't even make a pass at me.'

As I was leaving, she said, 'Sometime let's have supper here and go to a movie.'

'Michelle would like that,' I said.

Her eyes swerved away from mine. 'Of course, bring her. I like your wife.'

On the way out of the city, I drove by her apartment. I thought I saw her watching for me from out of the window and waved at what turned out to be a curtain which was furling from the heat of the radiator. During the drive home, I thought about the day we had lunch together, about the day she exploded into the restaurant and took off her sweater and afterwards when the old bum interrupted what was certain to be a passionate kiss which would eventually lead us into an affair. The old bum's remark–rather my own reaction to that old man watching us while he swore at the pigeons–was the single moment in which I had made up my mind about Laura Moore. I knew that if it had been Michelle, we would have kissed, whether the old bum was there or not.

So, I was glad that Michelle agreed to supper at Laura's and a movie after. We met in town one evening, but arrived at Laura's too early. Peter was just finishing a practice session.

Laura drew us aside. 'He isn't practicing hard enough,' she said to Michelle and me.

Peter stopped playing just as Laura said, 'Daniel, you talk to him. He respects you. Make him work harder.'

This was none of my business, no matter how intimate Laura and I had become over the past months. I saw how our intimacy disturbed Michelle and ignored it.

Peter turned away from the piano and looked at me, his eyes dull now and vacant.

'What am I supposed to say?' I asked Peter.

'We have to do something,' Laura said. 'Maybe I'm not a good influence on him. Maybe I'm bad for his work.'

'That's nonsense, Laura,' I said. 'You're a marvellous influence on everyone.'

'Then, let him tell you. Go on, Peter. Tell him. Tell him how you come home from your teacher more despondent each time. You know the Mozart hasn't gotten any better.' She whispered to me, her voice suddenly harsh, 'He blames it on his fingers. I'm beginning to think it's me and not his fingers at all.'

Michelle was silent. She was standing as far away from the piano as she could, not realizing how used Laura and I were to such talk. We had grown increasingly frank with one another over the past months, almost without realizing it.

Though Peter's eyes revealed nothing, nevertheless, his playing did. If you were to compare the sonata he played now to the way he played it a few months earlier, you could safely say that he had regressed. Each note was too singular. The flow and lyricism he had been trying to accomplish had vanished almost entirely. He was banging out the piece, banging it out with defiance. The music sounded as if it held an emotion almost contrary to the one Mozart had intended. In fact, he was murdering the Mozart and was, at the same time, damaging himself.

When he finished, with the discordance still alive in the room, he said. 'There, Laura, do you see? I have to go back. I can't do a damn thing here.'

Laura offered Michelle and me a drink while she and Peter finished talking in the kitchen. From the front room, we heard sobs. Soon, they were quiet and Peter left the apartment.

Michelle said we should leave, but I only wanted to be alone with Laura and went into the kitchen to be with her while she cooked. I admit to ignoring my wife that night, I admit I made her feel like an intruder and, in a sense, she was.

By the time we sat down to Laura's wobbly and bland tomato aspic, I was dizzy from the drinks. I drank too much wine at dinner and weaved up Commonwealth to the movie with a woman on each arm. I insisted on paying for Laura's ticket and, by doing so, decided that I was entitled to sit next to her. I must have touched Laura and fondled her more that night than I ever had when she and I were alone. It was safer, somehow, with Michelle there. Drunk, I had no perception of how foolish I looked and was only vaguely aware that I was wounding Michelle. After the movie, I walked Laura to her door and kissed her. She did not respond to my kiss. My arms went around her, but Laura's hands, like two white birds, remained quietly at her side.

Michelle had to drive home. Near Danvers it began to snow, fat sticky flakes which turned almost immediately to slush. I pressed my face against the window and watched it snow. Michelle sat perfectly straight, gazing out of the windshield. There was nothing to say, not at the moment, absolutely nothing to say.

At home, I made a drink. The thought of more to drink made me sleepy. I picked up my glass and lurched forward. 'Here's to Laura,' I said.

'Please don't act any more stupid than you are,' said Michelle.

Her look of disgust made me wish I had been quiet. I went into the yard, taking my glass. I didn't want to be with her. I wanted to be with Laura. It was cold and snowy, and I noticed from the soft glow that the moon was full above the clouds. I thought about the remark my secretary had made to me about lovers in the fall. But Laura was not my lover. Maybe I had embarrassed her.

It was too cold to stay outside very long, but before I returned into the kitchen, the shame and embarrassment became anger. I faced Michelle as an enemy. She ignored my glum mood and silence. She waited for an explanation, or a scene, or for me to apologize. Not a chance. I knew I had lost that battle long ago. So, I sat in silence, hating my wife for showing me that I could not have love both ways. I knew it. I had to accept it, seethed with anger. I hated her for showing the powerful morality under which we live; I hated myself for buckling under the morality.

Michelle, who was expecting if not an explanation then at least an outburst cornered me in the bathroom.

'I don't want to talk about it,' I said. 'Let it cool off. We'll only say things we'll regret.'

'Fine,' she said. 'Whatever you say.'

'Whatever you say,' I mimicked her.

'I don't know by what right you have to be angry. You

should be something else–not angry. You hurt me tonight, Daniel. I felt dumb and unwanted.'

'I'm sorry for that. That's my fault.'

'And you embarrassed me. I think you embarrassed her too. You had too much to drink. You acted like a little boy. I've never seen you act like that before. It made me ashamed.'

I couldn't explain it to her now. She was too hurt just then to want to try and understand me. I had no intention of hurting or of embarrassing anyone or of making her, especially her, feel unwanted.

The last time I went to Laura Moore's for lunch Peter was thoroughly distracted. At one point, he removed his coat and necktie and Laura excused herself to change out of her long dress to put on Levis and a man's shirt. It was odd. The formality among us disappeared as easily as that. In fact, half way through the meal, I excused myself and went into the living room to remove my own coat and necktie and to roll up my sleeves. Peter ate very little. What he did eat, he ate hurridly and instead of practicing he left.

I waited for Laura to do the dishes and suggested that we take a walk along the Charles. Probably, I should have let well enough alone and returned directly to the office.

We went down Commonwealth and down Arlington towards the river. From that point, the sailboats always look like soaring gulls. It was spring by that time. We crossed over Storrow Drive and found a clean, grassy spot. A couple, one much younger than ourselves, was lying on towels and gazing at one another. The entire time we sat there–not more than twenty yards from the water–the couple did not stop their kissing and caressing. It was impossible not to watch them. At one point, I remarked about how impressed I was by the young man. 'He can hold himself off quite well,' I said. 'She's been touching him for hours.'

'Quite possibly he isn't,' said Laura. And the blush on her face caused one to rise on my own.

'We were like that once,' I said.

'Of course we were,' she said. 'Do you think I can ever forget that?'

Then, I discovered there was really nothing more to say.

'This is one of my favorite things to do,' she said, after a time. 'To sit with someone by the river.'

We had seen very little of each other after the disasterous night at the movies. She seemed to be thanking me for returning to my old self.

'Me too,' I said, hoping my lie was not too transparent.

Anyone who saw us that spring afternoon would have assumed that we were lovers meeting in the middle of the day. We laughed briefly like lovers do. We held hands. I brushed her hair out of her face and touched a button on her shirt. But the curious thing about all of it was that there was no sexual impulse between us. We weren't holding ourselves back because of any consideration for Michelle or because of Laura's Peter. I probably know Laura Moore as well as I know anyone in the world, but nothing kindled between us then. It was as if we had had our kindling and now we had something else, something that the couple we watched didn't have.

We left the river. The couple was now lying close. We looked at them and then at each other, knowing that we were them once.

I don't know why I said it. Possibly, I'll never know for certain. It was barely a five minute walk back to Laura's apartment and I could have used the time for something other than to end whatever it was Laura and I had started. The tone of my voice, as I remember it now, was bitter. I sounded as if I were reprimanding her as well as myself. But I couldn't change my tone anymore than I could hold back what I had to say or disguise my disappointment. A mood had settled itself onto me and I had to talk my way out of it. 'It's confusing,' I said. 'I want to love you, Laura, but I can't.' I spoke quickly, I think, driving the words with my fist. As I spoke, she slowed her pace and bent her head. I couldn't see her face or know the effect of my words. 'I want to, but I can't. How many times I've thought of it.' On and on I talked, it did not occur to me that she might not have wanted me or that I had been a help to her–a catalyst in her freeing herself from Peter Salisbury–and I did not see her face or know, until it was too late, that I had made her cry. The restrictions of my way of life turned in me like a knife and I could not stop the flow of bitterness. Laura had done nothing. 'It's not that you aren't beautiful and kind. You are. To me, to everyone who looks at you. I want you to understand. I'm not allowed to love you. I am not allowed.'

At her apartment, she ran up the steps. I heard her moan as she threw herself against the door and realized only then that I had injured her, injured her without cause. As I walked away, I felt my strength draining; it was as if my feet had been knocked out from under me and I was suspended for a moment before I came crashing to the earth. And, I thought, quite possibly she is even more alone than I am. The victim. Possibly, she never felt any love at all, not the slightest, for me. Curious, yes; flattered, yes, by fawning, by attention; no, not love.

That night I had a dream. I was sitting in the back seat of a strange, luxurious car. I couldn't determine the car's make, nor did I recognize the owner. We were parked on an unfamiliar street. Michelle opened the passenger's door and handed the driver a box, a hand painted tin box which held marmalade. The driver took the box and leaned to kiss her.

'Oh, my darling,' Michelle said. 'You don't have to thank me. Not ever.'

Then, she turned the man's face towards her own and looked into his eyes. I saw how her eyes shone with love. I couldn't look away in time and watched her kiss him. I actually felt her kiss and the warmth of her affection, her softness, her melting. A shaft of sunlight glanced off her ring and I realized with a shutter, which was followed by a profound wave of sadness, that she was married to the strange man.

I sat rigid in the back seat. The love in Michelle's eyes completely overpowered me, as did the sensation which followed, making me feel sadder still. If only–something happened to me which had not happened since I was young. The sadness of my dream brought me awake. Frightened, I lay in bed. The dream, her love-filled eyes, her hands on a strange man's cheeks, all retained their vividness. Fully awake now I said aloud, 'If only *I* were married to her.'

I sat up then not realizing where I was. It was cold, but I sat erect, shivering. I must have remained in that position for a full minute before I realized that I was in our bedroom in our bed and that I was still married to Michelle who lay sleeping next to me, buried under the quilt. My relief was too great for me to resist pulling back the quilt to expose her head and neck.

'What do you want?'

I couldn't find her lips or her cheek in the tangle of hair and kissed the back of her neck. Anything. The feel of my lips on her flesh. She turned over in her sleep and I kissed her lips.

'Ummmm,' she said.

In the morning, I apologized for waking her, and she said that she didn't remember if I had.

The last time I saw Laura Moore was not too different from the first time. I was pushing through the turnstile at the Copley Square MTA stop to catch the subway for the bus station. A crowd had gathered at the far end of the platform, surrounding an old woman whose skirt was hiked up to her swollen white knees. She lay on her back with her eyes closed. A shopping bag was beside her, spewing groceries.

'Stand back. Please stand back,' someone was saying. 'Let her breathe. Won't all of you please stand back.' Of course, it was Laura in her paint-spattered levis and t-shirt, and the crowd responded to her calm authority. Then, I backed away, not because I was forced to do so by the crowd, but because I didn't want her to see me. My train rumbled into the stop, and from the window I saw Laura was still there holding off the crowd, continuing to console the dazed woman, who was now able to sit and embrace her shopping bag. Laura had her arm around her, steadying her.

On the way home on the bus that night, I sat next to Nelson Greenleaf. We shared the paper and I fell asleep between Boxford and Towlesport. I have always thought that the saddest thing about parting is when you roll up your rug, carry away your jade plant, your records, your books and take them back for your own use once more, because objects tend to hold the other person long after he is gone. Laura, I knew, would take some of Peter Salisbury home with her to Minnesota, and Peter would take some of Laura Moore with him to Paris, where, I hoped, under his old piano teacher he would play better.

Tonight, as I fell asleep on the bus, I didn't fall asleep thinking about Laura Moore, rather I thought about the old woman, unhinged on the subway platform. Though I continue to look for Laura, hoping that one morning soon I'll see her unloading a U-Haul near my office, the truth is that I cannot imagine a life different from mine now. No matter how hard I pretend, I can imagine no different life, not even one with Laura. If I had made my life with her, I'm certain that now I'd be riding home on some other commuter bus considering some other, some woman previous to Laura, with whom I once lay by some river somewhere in the world and looked at the gulls and the sailboats, because it wasn't each other we were interested in that afternoon when we watched those two lovers caress; we weren't at all interested in each other, at least not as we are now. So, I must let Laura Moore leave my thoughts.

Now, at least, I know what to do if someone collapses next to me. I have promised myself to respond just as I saw Laura respond–quickly, without fear and with authority, comforting the dazed old woman, holding off the crowd until help arrives–but, I must let even those thoughts go now, as well. We are in Towlesport. As always, the bus will discharge Greenleaf and me and a few others at the top of Cottle's Lane. It is, as I say, a five minute walk down the road to my home.

Staking
Claims

LOUISE BOARDMAN was an Eastern girl. Her thoroughly private education and her stoic New England heritage brought to her the courage and the sturdiness of a modern-day pilgrim. Once she understood how easily her life could turn out to be like that of her mother's and her mother's friends–an imposing old house, a country club, stale parties, a nanny much like her own for her children, a husband with prep school hockey scars, a closet full of shoes–she felt the pilgrim's longing for something fresh, for a different life. She began to look for someone improbable and found Tom Larkins. He was a local boy who lived near the lake in New Hampshire where her family had a summer home. And she let him get her pregnant. He was tall and handsome and his parents were Baptists.

Louise knew they would be out of place in her town and didn't want to live in his. So, they struck a solution which seemed to them both imaginative and full of adventure. They packed their wedding presents into his half-ton pick-up and drove west. For the trip, Louise wore a long calico skirt and a white blouse trimmed with lace. Her white wool socks were turned over the laces of her hiking boots. Her hair was piled in a casual swirl high on her head. The young groom wore a leather jacket trimmed with fringe, Levis with a button fly, and a stetson hat, which he peaked at the crown. It had a silver tooled hat band studded with fake turquoise.

The further west they drove, the more his accent changed. He began to tell her about things she'd never heard of–staking a mineral claim, diamond hitches, carbide lamps, sheepherder stoves. His dog rode in the truck bed with the wedding presents.

Near DuBois, Pennsylvania, the fuel pump broke and they were towed into town where Larkins locked the dog in the cab so he wouldn't be stolen. He left their belongings in the back of the truck for the night. 'Where we're going, we'll need a dog more than silver tea pots,' he told her, pulling his hat low over his forehead.

Outside of Toledo, Ohio, they detoured off the turnpike, looking for open country. The first gas station they came to was run by two young women in skin tight pants. The tape deck

in the office was playing 'Pussy Cat, Pussy Cat, I love you . . .
Love your pussy cat smile . . . Love to kiss your pussy cat lips.'

'Hot damn,' Larkins said, as they drove away with a full
tank. 'I never knew what that damn song was about before
now.'

They were far from home. She stiffened when his hand went
deep between her legs.

At a DX station somewhere in Iowa on the interstate, the
owner was chasing what looked like a dog. Louise asked the
owner the breed.

'Coyote.'

To Louise, the puppy seemed suddenly dangerous. The
owner picked up the coyote pup. Though he handled it gently,
it squealed in panic, shrill yelps echoing off the side of the
cinderblock building. 'Why not turn the little bastard loose?'
her husband said to the owner. 'Let it go its own way.'

On Route 70, in Kansas, they developed carburetor trouble.

The balled right front tire blew out in Castle Rock,
Colorado.

On Poncha Pass, outside of Salida, Larkins patched a burst
radiator hose with adhesive tape.

In Rio Cojos, Colorado, a shack and sagebrush town, the
transmission dropped onto the street. 'That's all she wrote,
Babe,' Larkins said.

They got a push to the Shell station, an adobe and board
building with two pumps out front. The owner, a thin, gnarled
man called Elmer Gill, claimed he couldn't do a thing for them.
'My tools was stolen,' he said.

'I've got my own tools,' said Larkins.

'You're welcome to use the lift,' said Elmer Gill.

Rio Cojos is shaped like a broken wagon wheel. At what
would be the hub of the half wheel is a sulfur hot springs. The
streets of the town radiate from the hot springs like spokes. The
outer boarder of the town, Route Nine, curves in a semi-circle
to form the wheel's rim.

For their first few months in Rio Cojos, Louise and Larkins
lived at the Pine Crest Motel. Louise cleaned rooms to pay for
their own. Larkins apprenticed himself to a locksmith. He

worked slowly and with precision, but refused to answer night calls for mislaid door and car keys. He talked his way into a free lance mechanic's job at Elmer Gill's Shell station. The upstairs of the office was a small apartment–kitchen, bedroom, bath. Larkins moved his wife there rent free when, in February, Louise was seven months pregnant and found cleaning rooms too exhausting. Her child, Bradley, named after her father, was born in the little clinic in Salida in April. Dotty, her childhood nanny, sent her a knit cap and mittens in blue. Her mother shipped out a large box of clothes, but hesitated to visit.

That summer, Louise took her old job back, cleaning rooms at the Pine Crest. In the fall, she began working the split-shift as a waitress at the Lobo Bar and Grill for more pay. Each morning, Louise left early to serve breakfast, taking Bradely to Mrs. Thurlow's where he spent his time on her living room floor surrounded by cats.

Bradley was always more interested in staying at the station with his father. In fact, he was so insistant one morning that Larkins did not open the station. Instead, they all went fishing north of town at a chain of beaver dams on Greasy creek, up by Elmer Gill's turquoise claim. The mountain peaks were snow covered by then, but the dams were open and alive with trout.

'There's a good cast,' Larkins said, talking over his shoulder to his son, who had refused to stay on shore with his mother and now slumped in his baby carrier. 'Simply great.' He landed the fly directly over a feeding trout. The fly, a ginger quill, bobbed naturally. 'Quiet now,' he said to his son.

Louise stood ankle deep at the edge of the pond, watching. The surface film and the light wind made the fly move. The water was too still for him to jiggle the fly without attracting attention to the line and leader.

She saw a large, experienced trout angle below and rise from the depths of the pool. Her heart quickened. A black shadow. The dorsal broke and the sun shot off the tail. A swirl. His fly sunk. 'A rainbow.' Louise yelled. 'They're biting.'

Larkins waded deeper into the pool and false casted, letting his fly dry before he put it down a yard or so from where it had landed on the previous cast. 'That was a huge one, Tommy,' she called to him.

Larkins took off his hat and flapped it at her. 'Be quiet. God damn it! Get away, if you can't shut up! I'm trying to fish, you dumb bitch. It's bad enough with him on my back.' He retrieved his fly and immediately set it down again, having dismissed her.

The burning sensation on her cheeks and neck receded slightly as she walked up the hillside out of sight. Soon, she had gathered enough wood for the lunch and was occupied in trying to ignite it. It was a bright warm day, and she realized that they would probably have better luck if she weren't harping at them from the shore.

When she had the fire blazing and the picnic laid out, she went to the hilltop and looked down at them. By that time, they were far out into the center of the pond. While she stood there, she saw her husband lose his footing. When he went under with Bradley on his back, it took all of her will not to run to them and help them out. As it was, she waited, out of sight, until she was certain they both were safe.

Louise had fried onions and potatoes and made hamburger patties to cook over the open coals. It was quite some trick, Larkins told her as he grilled the meat, it was really something to cast to the end of the dam by the tangle of dead willows and aspen stumps with a wiggling child on your back. Still, Larkins had managed to catch three small rainbows which they decided to save for supper.

'I couldn't interest the old grand-daddy in the pool,' he said. 'After you left, I waded out. He lolled and warmed his back in the sun just out of my reach.' He was careful to explain he had not put out too much line for fear of snagging Bradley's skull with the fly. 'But it's better to leave him there for another time. I'll go after him in the spring.'

More than the fish, he told her, Bradley had been interested in the birds. Bradley spread his arms and arched his back in imitation, wiggling and kicking in his baby carrier. 'Birdies! Birdies!' he shrieked into the clear, bright sky. 'More, more birdies!' Larkins told her that while he was wading out into the pool after the big grand-daddy trout Bradley had waved his arms so hard that he had to grab onto a willow so not to be lifted right out of the water by his son's flapping, and Louise found she could laugh.

What Larkins did not tell her is what he did not know she had seen for herself. Bradley was flapping on her husband's back. Larkins was intent on the big trout. Once again she saw him lose his footing and go under deep. Somehow, thank God, Bradley slipped out of the baby carrier and Larkins got a hold of him and was able to keep his head above the surface while he kicked to the beaver dam at the end of the pool and scrambled out with them both coughing and choking and Bradley kicking with fury in his father's arms. When she asked why they were so wet, he told her only that they had gone for a swim. And they smiled at the little boy, who was stripped of all but his shoes, his bare skin almost blinding in the intense sunlight, as he chased grasshoppers and startled small birds while the clothes dried in front of the fire.

At one time, Elmer Gill would repair cars as well as pump gas, but with Larkins working full time he did little more than restock the candy case and attempt to keep the books. But everyone knew that was an avocation. Elmer's real work was drinking whiskey. No one in Rio Cojos relied on Elmer Gill for anything except for a taste from his bottle now and then. Rather than tease or pity Elmer, most everyone dismissed him–whiskey being an occupational hazzard in a place like Rio Cojos. If Larkins had anything serious to talk to Elmer about, he found it best to catch him between eleven and four. He would be too moss headed before that and too thick tongued later. Kitty Gill looked after her father's interests. She double checked the accounts and made certain he did the assessment work on his mining claim each year, so not to lose it.

At that time, Larkins was virtually running the station alone. He disliked pumping gas, but there was no rent to pay and promise of a bonus if he could make the station turn a profit.

In the beginning, Kitty seldom came into the station. But Larkins saw her almost everytime he stepped onto the street.

He might be ordering an engine tool in the hardware store, or out at the Arsenal (he didn't drink where his wife worked) or he might be walking up to the Texaco to swap a fan belt, and Kitty would pop up in front of him in tight pants like he'd sprung a trap. Even now, in her late thirties, she was still raven haired, thin, with large pale eyes which struck Larkins everytime with an unsettling visceral force. Even the most brief meetings, a casual wave, a glance from across the street was leading to just one place. It was bound to happen. Louise knew that. She saw he was drawn to her and knew he was bound to make a fool of himself over her sometime, but she believed she was in no position to prevent it.

Kitty came by the station two or three times a day. Sometimes she would sit with Larkins after supper. Sometimes she would have the fire going before they got downstairs in the morning. They would find her sitting by the stove with the account book spread on her lap, her blouse cut low and her hair pinned up to show the fragility of her neck. Her skin was pale, almost translucent, and the gay underwear she wore to make herself feel supple and young showed through like a stain.

Each morning, Louise would pray that Kitty Gill would not be down there sitting in front of the stove with her cheeks pink and her hair all pinned up, quiet and young looking, not first thing.

Oh, Lord.

Then, they descended the stairs.

'I've been here for hours,' Kitty said. 'Is it warm enough? Coffee's ready. I've turned on the pumps, but no one's been by yet. We've got Barney's jeep to grease and tune and–oh, inspection time. Everyone's going to want a sticker.' Kitty had a complicated set of maternal tricks which she used on him instead of girlishness. 'You are doing well for us, Tom. More than a hundred and fifty in gas alone yesterday. Daddy never did that well in a week.'

'It's the tourists,' he said. 'More and more all the time. Oh, the candy's low. Elmer's forgotten again. If you think of it–'

She held a ruler which she had been using to read across the columns of numbers in the station's account book. Abruptly, she stood and tapped his shoulder. The metal edge struck his collar bone and he felt a twinge of pain. The gesture was meant to be formal, ritualistic. And its seriousness startled Louise. 'You dear boy,' said Kitty, standing close to him. 'How silly you can be. But, aren't you running this place? Why does Daddy have to do it? Can't you call Fred Thurlow and put in a candy order? Yes?'

'I can do that,' said Louise. 'I have to take Bradley up there anyway.'

A truck pulled up to the pumps and honked.

When he came back inside and rang up the sale, Kitty was hugging herself and rocking from side to side as if to warm her large breasts. 'Oh! Oh, Louise. It's so safe to have a man working here. You know, he is saving the station for us. I don't know how I can thank you both. We would have lost it without you.' She closed her eyes and smiled. 'You do deserve a bonus.'

It went on like that all fall and winter. The confinement of the small office of the two pump Shell station pressed Larkins and the older woman together. At times, he felt foolish and weak. Or a meanness came over him. Once he went so far as to tell Louise how he dreamed of dragging that woman bodily into the dark grease pit and giving it to her as a man, now fully a man, and not as a hired lacky, giving her what she deserved from him as a man. When such a moment occurred, Louise saw it. Somehow she could feel his rage like she could acid and cold–and she deflected him. She praised his work. She cooled him off. She petted his lust while she watched him slowly regain the veneer of gentleness and propriety which he had moments before so violently shed.

In a way, Louise admired Kitty Gill. Her brazenness fascinated her. She felt no moral barrier between them, no superiority and even a little friendliness. Kitty's brutal femaleness was as close to decay, as dark an aberration as any Louise had known before. That's what her husband was drawn to. She saw that he longed to experience her darkness, her unselecting and frank sexuality. She didn't trust Kitty with her husband, nevertheless, the woman fascinated her.

Larkins had a black mark on his upper thigh where his sister had jabbed him with a pencil. While working at the station, it trippled in size and grew a cap. When he noticed the mark had doubled again into the size of a pencil eraser, it scared him.

The mole was deeply rooted, but the doctor at the clinic in Salida gave him a local and cut it out. While he recovered, Kitty pumped gas. She took reservations for lube jobs and oil changes. Louise continued working the split shift at the Lobo and Bradley spent his mornings and evenings with Mrs. Thurlow.

One night, while Louise was across the street finishing the dinner shift, she chanced to look across the street and saw two figures in their bedroom window. She felt herself become suddenly tingling hot all over and didn't notice it when her hand knocked over a bottle of watered-down ketchup, spilling it on the table cover. For the remainder of the evening, she served and cleared in a sort of daze. After she had the tables set for the next morning's breakfast, she went to Thurlow's to get Bradley. She was carrying him down the empty street when the 'Lobo Bar & Grill' sign went out. The mechanism, which caused the neon Indian to wave his arms, slowly wound down. The figure faced her. The pulsating colored lights continued to flash and the eyes continued to blink alternately, giving the Indian an ominous, almost knowing leer. In her arms, in his sleep, Bradley knocked her beaded headband and the bright feather at the back went askew. The light in their bedroom above the office was still on. Carrying her son, she climbed the stairs and stood in the doorway of their bedroom, looking at Larkins asleep naked on their bed.

'Da Da,' said the sleepy child.

Louise's face had drained of its color. There was an odor in the small room which was feminine, but not hers. 'Tommy? Are you awake?'

He looked up at her and quickly pulled the sheet into his lap, covering his nakedness. The wound in his leg had opened. 'It's early. What time is it?'

'You're bleeding,' she said. 'Who was here? Has anyone been here?' She spoke with her back to him while she fumbled for gauze and adhesive tape in the cabinet above the small kitchen

sink. The rum bottle on the bedside table was half empty.
'I guess I got drunk,' he said. 'I was sick in the bathtub.'
'There wasn't anyone here. Was there? You look awful.
Why? You don't usually drink that much.'
'My leg hurts. What do you mean was there anybody here?
What the hell do you think I am?'
The room was too small. Her son was present. There was a
stubborn tone to Larkin's voice. All of this made Louise relent.
A numbness filled her spirit and she felt a lassitude envelop her.
'I'm not mad or anything, Tommy. I just asked. That's all.'
She was suddenly so exhausted that she couldn't keep her eyes
open. 'I thought I saw someone earlier.'
   He looked at her and rolled onto his stomach to grab the
bottle off the bedside table and drink. He gagged once but was
not sick to his stomach. 'You thought wrong,' he said. He was
ugly then, and she looked away.
   The odor she had sensed when she first entered was no longer
present. But her torpor was, along with her certainty. 'I don't
want to talk about it any more tonight. I only made five dollars
in tips today. I'm too tired to care.'
   He drank again. She dressed her child for bed. Bradley had
been quiet the entire time, but now, as if he sensed his mother's
mood, burst into tears. Larkins went into the bathroom and
tried to clean out the tub and sink. Louise stood at the door
watching him struggle. In her shy, quiet manner, as she
removed her waitress uniform–beaded belt, moccasins with
arch supports, squaw dress, blouse–she told her dazed husband
that she thought she might be pregnant again. She told him
that she would rather not use disposable diapers this time or
use the Mexican woman's diaper service. There was plenty of
room in the garage for a washer and dryer. She said that she
was telling him early so he would have plenty of time to get
used to the idea of Bradley having a brother or a sister. 'Also,
we can still make love for a while. At least, I think it's all right.'
   While Louise washed herself and put on a nightgown, he
changed his bandage. 'Damn, another kid,' he said.
   As usual, before getting into bed, she knelt beside him. He
prayed aloud for them both. He swayed from side to side,

bumping her shoulder. By the time he finished, he no longer swayed, but leaned against her to hold himself up. When he stopped, she helped him to stand.

II

Early the following spring, Kitty Gill took Louise up to her father's turquoise claim. Located about eleven miles from Rio Cojos in Taylor Basin half way up Dead Indian Draw, the mine buildings–office and tool shed–were on Greasy creek a few hundred yards below the blasted shaft entrance. The most prominent sight was the huge piles of waste rock Elmer had bulldozed while trying to strip mine. Gray piles of clay like stone studded with turquoise nuggets. The office was barely habitable, but Elmer had set up a cookstove and drilled a well for the dry sink. The waste ran out into an open settling pond. The outhouse was set away from the office in a grove of aspen trees.

The massive dynamite charge Elmer had used to open the shaft for pit work had shattered the surface rock, reducing any turquoise to small blue droplets, which after a thunderstorm showed up as brilliant blue tears in the gray muck.

Kitty drove up there often to fill a coffee can with the small pieces, which the jewelry maker Ernie Hinkle bought.

On Louise's first visit to the mine, she and Kitty picked turquoise for a half an hour. When Kitty's back began to hurt, they went back to town. 'Ah ah. It gets me right there, doesn't it,' said Kitty arching her back and rubbing the base of her spine.

Louise was quiet.

They drove to the station and found Elmer, who'd agreed to watch the pumps for the afternoon while Larkins went to Salida for parts, nodding inside drunk. They woke him and waited while he fumbled with his bottle. He sipped a little to get his mouth unstuck.

Kitty showed him the turquoise. 'It took us just a half an hour to pick this,' she said, rattling the stones. 'It's worth what?

Twenty, twenty-five to Ernie?'

Groping for the can, heavy breathing, Elmer fingered a few stones. 'Mostly rotten. Polished and greased. He'll give you fifteen, maybe twenty.'

He struggled to stand. Weaving in the middle of the office, he polished off the whiskey. Kitty and Louise were used to that by now. Louise assumed he did it because he felt guilty for not picking the turquoise himself.

'Daddy, I don't want to say anything,' Kitty said, 'I know it's none of my business. But, you're trying to kill yourself. I don't want that.'

Elmer didn't look at her.

'It's like living with two people. You drunk and you sober. I like you better sober. You're hardly that way anymore.'

Elmer jerked and bumped the cash register, sideswiped by the whiskey. Then, they exchanged the first significant glance in months. Without a word, Elmer put on his coat and took a few bills from the register. She steadied him as they walked to the jeep. Before she got in on the driver's side, she asked, 'It will be a month. Do you want to take anything, I mean, to get you there?'

Elmer shook his head. 'There's a pint in the glove box,' he mumbled, thick tongued.

A few days later, Kitty explained to them that Elmer would be back from the sanatorium in Colorado Springs by the middle of May. She wanted Larkins to help Elmer with the assessment work on the claim for that year.

'The Lord must want us to be miners,' Larkins said to Louise later that afternoon. 'He's dropped this right into our laps. I don't want to talk about it anymore.'

'I refuse to fight with you,' she said. 'I'll go. That's the end of it.'

'I don't want to fight anyway.'

'I didn't think you did. We won't stay up there too long. Will we?'

'I don't know. A few months. Where did you hide the rum?'

'Above the sink behind the Clorox.'

'I didn't think you'd tell me.'

'I didn't either.'

'You don't like me very much. Do you?'

'Not when you drink I don't.'

Larkins tilted his hat onto the back of his head and poured himself a half a glass of rum. He raised his glass to her. 'Here's to turqouise,' he said. 'I'll see you later.'

Louise put on her waitressing uniform and went across the street to serve dinner. By the time she finished her shift, she had papered the walls of the mine office and, in her mind, hung curtains in the windows and could visualize Bradley, short and sturdy, with a little pick on his shoulder and a small miner's helmet on his head.

In the office, Larkins had drifted away. He slept in the overstuffed chair. He had not removed his hat. She turned off the television and went upstairs to begin a letter to her parents. By nature, Louise was not a correspondent. Her tendency was to write home when she wanted something. Now, Louise didn't want a tangible object. She wrote to cheer herself up. If there was any hint of unhappiness or of stress or uncertainty, she did not intend it.

'. . . So, we're to be miners for the summer,' she wrote. 'It's hard unyielding land about eleven miles from Rio Cojos in a small valley which has steep sides like a wedge has been removed from a mountain. You follow a small stream up to a clearing. The first thing you see is the dump rock. There's a tool shed and an office where we'll live. Well, when I saw it, I thought no one could live there and be comfortable. This afternoon, I had a conversation with the Lord that went something like this: "Lord, if you want us to live in a place like that all summer, then you'd better make it easy for us, because I'm not certain about quitting a good job in town just as the tourists have begun to come through to live way up there in the sticks like a rag-a-tag prospector's wife." Still, Tommy says he is going to put everything he has into this. Is he excited! For the first time, he is really looking forward to something.

'In a few weeks, Elmer will be back. We have agreed to do a minimum of one hundred dollars worth of assessment work by winter, so Elmer won't lose his claim. We'll move back here to the station for the winter. I may even waitress again. . . .'

In mid-May, when Larkins moved his family up to the mine, the snow patches still hung to the hillside and Greasy creek ran high and white. The deer, starving and unafraid came right up to the door of the mine office and ate almost anything Louise put out for them, including grape jelly from a jar. Their pink tongues reached deep and quick into the glass while they kept their eyes moving and their haunches tense, prepared to bound away at any threatening movement or harsh glance of light.

At first Kitty Gill rode up to the mine every day to supervise the work. One afternoon, Elmer caught Larkins watching the clean, well dressed woman get out of the jeep by the red gasoline drum. He went over to Larkins and nudged him in the ribs. 'You best watch that one,' he said. 'She eats up little fellars like you.'

Larkins eyed Elmer. 'Think so?'

'I surely do.'

'Maybe.' Larkins watched her walk. There was something fresh about Kitty–not new-fresh or clean-fresh, more like used-car-fresh, OK Approved.

She talked with the men for a moment and went to find Louise. 'You must come and visit me sometime,' Kitty told her. 'I know. You're so busy here, you hardly get out. Well, do anyway.'

Nervous, Louise stoked the stove until the room was too hot. 'I will then,' she said.

It wasn't jealousy, she realized. It was mistrust. Louise had not been raised with women who played with other women's men, blatantly, at night and went about their business the next day as if nothing had happened. That's where the chill came from, she realized after Kitty had gone. Different rules. Out here the women live by different rules, ones which Louise had not encountered before–she didn't want to think about it anymore.

'It's me again,' she wrote to her parents. 'Tonight your grandson and I are going to devour with great relish and lust the first and most beautiful zucchini squash from our pitifully small but glorious garden. Tommy hates zucchini so we get it all. The peas went crazy. I had to pick almost all of them today. Peas, peas. We have a few tomatoes, too, They'll be ready soon. I've never had a garden before. I know, I did work in yours and had my own rows, but this is different. This one is all mine and when anything comes up, I have to tell everyone about it. Oh, I almost forgot. Elmer found us an ice box. It's at least eighteenth hand. I'm chewing on the first piece of ice to come out of the freezer. It works on bottled gas–I'm not sure how. The inside trays and drawers are pink and yellow and all neatly labeled–meat, vegetables, eggs. It has a knob inside the butter compartment for soft or hard, but it's mostly soft.'

By this time, she was almost seven weeks pregnant. She and her husband had not spoken of this since that night. Now, she decided not to mention it to her parents. Best to wait, she decided, until she began to show.

'I have been to the doctor for a check up,' she wrote. 'Tommy heard me coughing and proceeded to give me a half an hour's lecture on the dangers of cigarette smoking. I think he was disappointed when I informed him that I was not a secret smoker. But, it seems to me that of all people he would know if I did. Mrs. Thurlow is a secret smoker. She hides her cigarette ends in her bra. I always wondered why she smells. The doctor said I had the beginnings of bronchial pneumonia. It would have been cheaper to have gone right into the hospital, considering the doctor's bills and the pounds of medicine I had to buy aren't covered by the medical insurance Elmer took out for us. But that was weeks ago and I'm up and around speeding like a bullet, well a slow bullet. Tommy says I still smell like a hospital–I was only there four days. I know I should have called you, but all I would have been is sorry for myself. So, I'm all well now, thank the Lord for that, and feel pretty sparky . .'

She put the letter in her clothes box for the time being and began to shell peas.

The assessment work for that year, Elmer had decided, was to reshingle the tool shed, set up a second and larger turqoise washer (the chasis and barrel of an abandoned cement truck) and build an awning over the screen from which they picked turquoise. Elmer spent a great deal of time staking out a new road up to the mine. Larkins fulfilled his promise to himself and worked harder than he ever had in his life. Louise adapted to the woodstove and did the laundry by hand. Because of the cost of lime and the possibility of odor, no one of them was allowed to urinate in the out house. And her son enjoyed running around the place stripped to the waist relieving himself at will. Louise, herself seldom broke the out house rule. When she did, she always closed the door, depriving herself of the magnificent view down the valley to the plateau and the Sangre de Cristo Mountains beyond that.

She pumped up a pan of water. She poked at the fire in the stove. The noise of the washer outside, of rock tumbling in the huge revolving drum, filled the room, a space about four paces by five with a bare concrete floor. She was not yet used to the noise nor the smell of the place. In her mind, mines had no odor. But there it was. No matter what direction the wind came from, the turquoise washer's exhaust blew right into the office, making the blue muslin curtains which she had hung in front of the window holes flap.

Her husband was on the tool shed. Elmer, thinner than when he went to the sanatorium in Colorado Springs and not quite sober, was gassing the jeep from the large red tank by the road. Her son was asleep in his wooden box on the floor by their foam mattress. She added wood and closed the stove. Resisting the impulse to wake Bradley, she got her note pad and returned to her place–the small formica covered table by the sink. She cleaned away the pea shells and read what she had written before she continued:

'. . . I hope all of this doesn't sound too romantic! We are really very happy for now, considering all the work that has to be done. I think I'm glad we left the station for the summer. Tommy seems happier up here than he was, and I care about that. Once he and Elmer get the small muck pile by the office picked, they plan to haul the big washer up to the mine. Then it will be quiet around here. I never appreciated silence before now. It is such a relief when the washer stops at night and I can hear myself, Me, think. At night, Tommy and I are especially quiet. You can hear everything, because at this point in our lives there aren't any windows in the office. We might as well be sleeping outside on the ground. When we have the capital, we are going to pump out the mine shaft and start tunneling for turquoise like proper miners and stop being muck pickers.

'The water in the pit is low now and you can see the shaft opening. Elmer's blast exposed some veins that are so thick you can peel the turquoise off with a coffee spoon, but they break apart when you wash them. The blasting ruined most of the surface rock, but according to Elmer, when we tunnel, we'll find deep blue beautiful turquoise. The veins could be as thick as my arm, he says, and solid. Or even better, the veins might be spider-webbed with gold! Sometimes I get so impatient I stand at the edge of the pit tempted to dive in and swim along the vein and bring up a big piece worth maybe hundreds of dollars. This might be our big chance. . . '

While the large revolving barrel rumbled, buffeting away the clay-like slag that clung to the blue stone, Larkins hoisted package after package of shingles onto the tool shed roof. He was a dozen or so yards from the mine office, and she could see him through the window hole above the sink. He worked slowly with precision, lining up the shingles carefully, checking the overlap, fitting them snug. And she heard it when Elmer chided him about his painful sense of perfection.

'Why don't we gild her too,' Elmer yelled. 'You act like that roof's up there to stay.'

'Toss me some nails,' Larkins said without bothering to look up from his work.

It was hot and dry, and from her location she could see her husband's back, burned from the sun and glistening with sweat. She liked him better that way than dressed in blue overalls smelling like gasoline.

Elmer kicked at the sill of the shed. His toe sunk inches into the rotting aspen log. 'A roof that fine means replacing the sills.'

'I can do that. No reason to lose a good shed over rotten sills.' He continued to nail shingle after shingle in line. 'House jacks.

I'll need two house jacks.'

'I'm going to town anyway,' Elmer said.

Before Elmer left, he pulled his light blue jeep in front of the door and beeped. The horn jolted Bradley in his sleep, but he did not awaken. Elmer wanted to know could he bring anything back from town? Yes, milk and mayonnaise. And, yes, take the mail in.

She hurriedly signed off the letter she had been writing and searched her clothes box for postage.

'Forget it,' said Elmer. 'I'll stake you to the stamp.'

That was kind of Elmer, she said to herself. It would save her a trip into town later, but she had been stuck up at the mine for more than a week and was looking forward to going herself.

Louise checked her sleeping child. She couldn't seem to spend enough time with him. All her energy, it seemed, was used in keeping the place running. She was constantly either pumping water or keeping the fire up. What's worse, she said to herself, I don't feel badly about neglecting him. She took a pot of pea shells out to the rabbit cage. 'Well, Lord,' she said half aloud. 'If you could somehow tell me how to pay more attention to him, I would appreciate it.'

She didn't see Bradley, half awake now, stumble out into the sunlight. The slamming of the screen door must have awakened him. He wore no clothes. When Louise heard a soft plop and tiny cry for help, she ran around the woodpile and found Bradley face first in the settling pond. Her scream rose above the noise of the turquoise washer.

Larkins dropped to the ground and ran to them. Bradley was draped with green slime. Louise couldn't bring herself to hold him. She was afraid to give him mouth to mouth resuscitation. 'I can't. I'll blow his lungs out!'

'Cold,' Bradley said. Then, he started to cry.

Larkins carried him to the office and forced him under the pump. The cold water produced more screams. 'If you can't watch this kid, tie him up,' he said. 'What's going to happen when they're two of them?'

Louise was silent. She held out a towel. Larkins went to the refrigerator and made his own lunch which he ate by himself on the tool shed steps. A while later, she heard him working on the roof again. He would work until dark. The room was clean. The rabbits fed. The wood box full and the stove banked for the afternoon–draft and damper closed down. The breakfast dishes had been washed and put away. Diapers were soaking. Bradley was quiet now, playing with rocks in his toy corner. A light breeze made the curtains flutter gently. She had no desire to go outside.

III

After supper that night, she felt dizzy and lay in bed alone for what seemed like hours before she was quiet enough to try and sleep. Her husband had gone to town to play cards with Elmer and some other men. Louise was not sure whom he played cards with, but whomever it was a better gambler then her husband. Before she fell asleep, she decided that she needed to talk with someone. The only person she could think of was Kitty Gill. That was all right. Besides, they might become fast friends, anything was possible.

The following afternoon, she borrowed the jeep and, with Bradley, drove to Rio Cojos. The station was closed. Louise left Bradley with Mrs. Thurlow and called Kitty from the pay phone at the Lobo.

Kitty lived in a trailer south of town near the Arsenal Bar. Louise found her sitting spread legged on the couch at the end of the living area, exposing herself like a flower. She wore tight black slacks and a dark sweater. The floor was covered with Navajo rugs and the tables with squat black pottery bowls. San Ildefonso Pueblo, Kitty explained.

Louise couldn't decide if she liked Kitty. Nevertheless, after a cup of tea, she told her about the baby.

'How long has it been?'

'Almost two months.'

'How do you feel?'

'I've been having dizzy spells. It's nothing.'

'Are you sure you want it?' Kitty asked.

'I don't know anymore.'

'You have a choice, you know that. It's not too late.'

'I suppose I do.'

'Do what?'

'Know I have a choice.'

'Well?'

Louise was silent.

'For Christ's sake,' said Kitty. 'You need something to drink.'

The inside of the trailer was cool. Louise drank too fast. Relaxed, she enjoyed looking at Kitty stretched on the couch.

Later, in a daze of sherry, with a swamp in her belly, Louise felt a howl growing inside, womb deep and painful. The sherry bottle made another round and Louise's glass wavered under the pale golden stream. Kitty stopped at half a glass. When she motioned for Louise to come and sit next to her on the couch, Louise obeyed. When Kitty's hand fell on Louise's leg, a jolt passed through her.

'Well, when were you last touched? You should be surprised more often, Louise. You've got to learn to control that blush of yours.'

Louise took Kitty's hand away, commenting on how delicate her fingers were. She displayed her own large and rough hands. 'They weren't always this way.' When Louise went into the bathroom, she felt how her buttocks had expanded to fill out the stretched corduroy pants. In Kitty's mirror, she saw that her breasts in the old cotton brassier had lost tension, while Kitty's even without a bra retained their firmness. She wished she could make herself do something or change something to make herself attractive again. She was dizzy again and felt sick.

She sat next to Kitty. 'Your husband's very nice,' said the older woman.

'That's true, I guess.'

'And me?' Kitty asked.

Then, somehow it started. This time, when Louise felt a pressure on her thigh and the nails of Kitty's delicate fingers on her flesh, Louise colored but did not flinch. Kitty did not look at her. Like a small girl, Louise was afraid to resist. She was too dizzy to care. The trailer seemed too close, pushing the outside world away. There was only Kitty and herself. She didn't care. She couldn't see clearly, which made the patterns in the Navajo rug at her feet jump at her. Waves of nausea surged up in her. 'Shhh,' said Kitty. 'You're just upset.' Kitty edged forward on the couch and opened her legs wide, lifting herself on her heels. 'No,' said Louise. 'I think I'm sick.'

The howl now building in her belly crept up to her throat, sour and stagnant. The after taste of the sherry was like oil. Louise felt Kitty take her hand and hold it. 'It's not the sherry,' Louise said, faintly. 'I've felt it before. But not so strong.' And the howl–the silent scream–continued to build even as she tore her hand from Kitty's grip and turned her face away from Kitty's. For an instant her head cleared. Then a silent howl as intense as a noon siren exploded in her making her ears ring. Louise stood, turning away from Kitty to hide her sobs. When she regained control of herself, with the howl still flooding her ears, she fled from the trailer, leaving Kitty collapsed on the couch like a wingless angel in black.

The pressure continued to build. It's intensity made her face twist. It was a noise as loud and as piercing as any scream, but it could not be heard by the sulphur springs down town. It did not wind down the isles of Chuck Swanson's hardware store nor wake Bradley from his nap in Mrs. Thurlow's bedroom. The deafening howl of rage and sorrow which had emerged from the swamp in Louise's belly was audible only to Louise. Blindly, she drove to the Shell station and let herself in where she stumbled upstairs. The bed was stripped of everything but the mattress cover. She stripped and put on an old shirt of her husband's she found in the closet. She covered her ears and swayed on the bed. The howl remained.

Larkins found her later in the day. She wanted no one to stay with her. She wanted no food. Larkins could arrange for Bradley to spend the night with Mrs. Thurlow. She had to cover her ears to speak, but even then she could hardly hear her own voice.

Louise spent the night alone on the white mattress cover in the bare room above the station. Later, to save the bed, she moved onto the floor where she watched the redness move on the absorbent cloth like ink on a blotter, dampening both it and her flesh and drying dark. She was conscious of what was happening to her and that the bleeding would stop and that she had not been so far along that she was in any physical danger. She sat erect on the white mattress cover, rigid. The howl was still like blood in her ears and an anvil's ring.

She awoke when her husband came into the station the next morning and she directed her rage at him through the floor. She sat up when she heard him on the stairs and made no move to cover herself, wanting him to find her, blaming this on him, believing him to be the cause.

And he found her in his old white shirt sitting on the floor, small and pathetic.

'I've been bleeding . . . a little.'

'That means . . .' He patted his pockets searching for his pipe.

'Oh, Lord! I know what it means.'

'I'll get a doctor.'

'No. No, it takes care of itself.'

'Are you sure? How bad is it?'

'How bad?' She lifted the front of the shirt. 'I wanted this baby,' she said. 'I wanted it. Do you believe that?'

'Sure, Babe. Something went wrong.' He started to go toward her.

'No. I don't want you to touch me.'

'It might have been undeveloped or sick. Your body discharged it. That's all, Babe. Your belly went bad. You can try again.'

'That's callous.'

'If there wasn't something wrong, this wouldn't be happening.'

'You can't be that clinical.'

She had covered the redness again, but almost wanted to strip to let him see for certain the new brilliant pool of redness she felt, like a warm haze growing around her.

'Hey, I'm not trying to make you angry.'

'I wanted this baby,' she repeated, but to herself. 'I thought it would help us.'

He lit his pipe.

He was relieved. She could see that by the way he smoked. 'Maybe the kid wasn't strong enough.' He puffed. 'After all, what are you? You are only the vessel.' He puffed again. 'The Lord knew the cargo was damaged, so . . .'

'You bastard!' Now, she did rip open the shirt to make him see all the slickness. Eyes blazing, lips pressed tight, she held the shirt open. Buttons rolled across the floor. After a time, she spoke to him in a low, harsh voice. 'You just shut up and leave me alone. Go back to your mine. I don't want you in the same room with me. The Lord! Truth! You bastard! You–you, selfish pitiless bastard!'

'You're just upset,' he said. He put his pipe in his coat pocket and left, carrying the television set. 'I'll stay downstairs for a while. Call me if you get hungry.'

Soon, the toilet flushed. Louise called him as 'The Wheel of Fortune' came on the television.

She sat on the bed supported by caseless pillows. She pointed to it on a piece of dark stained tissue. 'There,' she said. 'You look at it. There's the cargo. I'm not pregnant anymore.'

She, herself, had not looked at it carefully. Nor would she examine it later through the peanut butter jar when she took it to the clinic in Salida. She knew no more about it, would never know anymore about it than this: it was a small, dark clot. Her hands shook when she passed it to the nurse to be tested.

Now, she felt only a pin prick in her belly. The howling had stopped. She still wore the old white shirt open at the front. Her hair was matted and stuck to her forehead and cheeks. 'I would like to eat. May I please have some food and a glass of water. If it's not too much trouble. I would like a blanket and some sheets. I'm cold.' She felt his hand on her arm and opened her eyes to see him look away from the darkness on the tissue, away from the blood on her thighs, away from the stained mattress cover on which she had been sitting, out of the window.

'I've lost my baby!' Now, she could cry.

He left her for a few minutes to find the bed clothing. When she was comfortable, he got her lunch. She watched herself watching him carry the tray. 'I got it at the Lobo,' he said.

'Chicken fried steak.' His eyes were small and red-rimmed from lack of sleep. He looked bent. Her howl had penetrated all right, she saw that. He appeared to her-standing there with his shoulders sagging, as he would years later-broken and aged. 'Canned peas. Mashed potatoes with mild gravy. Hot rolls and butter.'

She was silent.

'You must eat.' He sounded practical rather than sympathetic. 'So, what do I do with it?' He referred to the darkness on the tissue beside her pillow.

'Get a clean jar. I have to get it tested. Put it in the refrigerator.'

'I can do that,' he said, setting the tray on the bed.

She leaned forward while he adjusted her pillows. 'Thank you, Tommy.' She discovered that she was fascinated by the old man who was nursing her, fathering her. She wished he would never go away, that the veneer of the kind old gentleman would remain and that her husband, that man she knew underneath would not surface again.

Louise remained in bed for almost a week after the bleeding stopped and the howl had crept back down her throat into the swamp in her belly. She left the windows open to keep out the smell of grease and gasoline which seeped up through the floor. She lay quietly in bed, mending, changing, determined that for as long as he appeared to, pretended to, care, she would stay with him. Their love would be expedient and practical, not romantic. Still, that was a kind of love nonetheless. After all, they had a child to raise. Theirs would be from now on and forever a love based entirely upon her will to survive and would last for as long as Larkins cared for her. Though she was silent inside, though the horrible noise had stopped, her eyes now held a certain wildness, a fear and disappointment, which she had never felt before. Physically, she felt all right. The dizziness was entirely gone. Yet, she was filled with rage-only rage-deep, embittered, sad rage. She felt no kindness towards him anymore. It was ridiculous to think of kindness now, or of love. She wondered only if she would ever be able to speak to him again, to speak to him as she had in the past, from her heart, and not as she did now, from habit–remote and polite. But, if he continued to care, or to pretend to care, she decided that it meant, at the very least, that he respected her and so loved her enough. If he did respect her, if she could depend on his continuing respect, then that was enough. In fact, she decided at last, that was quite more than enough.

IV

So, Louise moved back up to the mine, and love–in a way–did fill the small mine office. In a few days time Louise caught up to and overcame the weeds in her garden. Her husband had not forgotten to feed her rabbits. The office needed a thorough cleaning. Elmer had stayed with Larkins while she was away and the volume of cans and empty bottles was enormous. They had spent a small fortune in booze and beans. She fell once again into the routine of wood, rabbits, stove, pump and so on. Finally, one afternoon, she felt stable enough to write home.

She had firmly decided not to speak of her miscarriage. It was over now. Past. Besides, there is no shame in losing a baby.

'Hi! It's me. The sun is going down which means it's nearly four o'clock. Tommy took the watch with him. He and Elmer have gone to New Mexico to look at another mine. They're after tips. We could use a few. I don't know when they'll be back, so as I'm writing this, I'm listening for the jeep at the same time. It could get sort of lonely and scary up here at night alone. Other women have been left alone in the mountains like this, some even spent winters alone and made it (most of them anyway). What I really should be doing is the cleaning . . .' The light in the office was dim and she lit a kerosene lamp. 'I haven't thanked you for the check for the washing machine,' she continued. 'Before we found one that had a gas motor, Tommy found a kit to make a real Kentucky black powder rifle and a bullet mold. I can wash clothes just as well in the galvanized tub I have been using, but could use a washboard. There's a special black powder hunting season next month, before the regular season opens. I don't mind the idea of his shooting a deer, especially after what happened to my garden a few mornings ago. The rifle will pay for itself with one deer, where as a washing machine only uses up gas. Also, thanks for the box of clothes. Now, Bradley and I have something to wear that isn't patched over the patches.

'For Tommy's birthday, I have decided to make him leather hunting pants with Davy Crocket fringe and a pouch for a hunk of turquoise. Turquoise is supposed to protect you from accidents and to improve your aim. He practices every night and is getting a little better. . .' She had come to the end of her note pad. Now, she turned the pad over and sat for a moment, quietly thinking, searching for a fresh thought. She began writing on the backs of the sheets. 'Here's my latest and brightest, dumb idea. I thought Tommy would kill me. But, there's a ranch five miles down the road toward Rio Cojos and no one has lived there for years. I thought that I could stay home and Tommy could catch a ride up here with Elmer in the mornings. We'd be out of the way, and I could begin to build something. But, as it is, we barely get along without paying rent, so how would we pay for any improvements on the place with rent payments added? Anyway, he hasn't killed me yet over this. He just thumbs through his Bible and makes me listen to all of the parts he can find about how a wife should be somewhat more submissive to her husband than I tend to be. For the last week, I have been silent about the ranch. Absolutely close mouthed. I think it has been the hardest thing I have ever done. Of course it's not practical. Nothing will grow down there without a well. Wells cost a lot out here. Still, we could raise chickens. It's so close, Tommy could even walk to work. My plan is to find an old wooden tank and haul water in someone's truck and put a roof over the tank to keep the water fairly cool. I snuck inside the cabin the other day. It's empty, so we could move right in. I bet it is almost as large as this place. It has a dirt floor and not a cement one. But, the dirt is hard and as polished as linoleum. And, it would be quiet. But, as I've said already, I may be thinking about it, but I haven't breathed a word on this topic. I have had my mouth absolutely shut. . . .'

She was about to describe the furnishings—the rusty box

stove and the rough board shelves and the pole bunk—when she heard the high pitched whine of the jeep working its way up the valley. Quickly, she collected her papers and put them in her clothes box and found her Bible. She wanted to be reading the Bible when Tommy came home, not writing or sleeping.

The following day at noon, she woke Bradley from his morning nap and fed him to have him out of the way. She tied him with a length of rope to the door of the jeep and called the men for lunch.

As if Elmer had heard her thoughts of the night before, he said to her, 'I haven't any idea what it would cost to make that place down there liveable. I drove in there this morning. It was hot as blazes even then and no place for a youngster. They're snakes in the cabin. Let us pray.'

Automatically, they responded.

'Thank you, Lord,' said Elmer. 'For the good weather we've been having these past few days, and for the stone that has begun to show up on the screen, and for these bountiful sandwiches we are about to receive in Your name. For the love of Christ, our Savior, we pray. Please keep the snow back for a few more weeks and us all in good health and sane acting. Amen.'

That last referred to Louise and to hide her embarrassment, she turned to the sink and grasped the pump handle. Through the window hole, she saw Bradley crying and struggling, trying to stretch his harness. The washer blanketed his voice, but she saw the frustration and helplessness on his face and wondered, briefly, if it mirrored her own.

'You tell me,' said Elmer to Larkins. 'Should I start looking for a new man?'

Her husband's mouth was full. She heard the muffled negative. He shook his head and swallowed, pointing his thumb at her. 'She thinks it's what she wants.'

'Boy, you can't have it both ways.'

Usually, she didn't speak to them while they were eating. Now, her voice was clear but constricted. 'We can always try. What keeps us from trying, Elmer? Tell me that. If it doesn't work, we can move back up here.'

Elmer's chair scraped on the concrete floor. He wiped his mouth and put his napkin on his plate. 'I want to tell the both of you something. We are after a substance that goes all the way back to the Egyptians, probably a lot farther than that. It was more precious than gold to the Aztecs. What both of you seem to have forgotten is that we are not a bunch of rockhounds after geodes or dolimite.'

She listened with her back pressed against the sink. 'Tommy would still work here for you. I'd be down there. I could raise chickens, maybe.'

Elmer swung his gaze to her. He was dry looking, hollow almost.

'I—I just want a place to call ours,' she said. 'Where I don't have to tie up my boy. I just can't spend another winter in town. It gets too crazy in town in winter. Everybody is pushed too close together, and they act strange. You know that. Even Kitty gets strange in winter.'

Elmer looked at Larkins. The younger man's dark gaze was flat and cold like obsidian, revealing only stubbornness.

Elmer's teeth seemed to spark. There was no friendliness in his tone and he spoke low and privately. 'Blue gold,' he said. 'What we're after is blue gold. You can't name a better stone. To some it's more precious than diamonds.' He folded his hands. 'Let us pray. Thank you, Lord. Thank you for this meal she has prepared from the bounty of Thy larder. It will be more than sufficient to see me through 'til suppertime. Amen.' He snatched his hat from the counter. 'If you're working for me, Boy, let's get to it.'

As Larkins walked to the door, he stuffed the remainder of his sandwich into his mouth.

Louise followed the men outside and untied her son. When they revved the turquoise washer to dump another load onto the picking screen, she scooped him up and ran back into the office. Inside, she let Bradley go and covered her ears to block out the noise.

'Lord, it isn't that I don't appreciate the mine and all it gives us. It's just—just that I don't want Bradley to grow up here.' She pumped up the wash water. As she was filling her husband's clay water jug, the fragrance of sage hit her nostrils. She wiped her eyes and stood motionless, trying to fully capture the smell. A vision of winter came to her then. She could see her husband smoking his pipe. He read by the kerosene lamp from his leather covered Bible. A lake of moonlight shone through the tiny window at the end of the ranch cabin, shimmering on their bed. Bradley, still awake, sat straight in his sleeping box amazed by the red glow on the side of the rusty box stove. She was across the stove from Tommy. Her shoulders were covered with a black shawl. She was sewing. No. She wasn't sewing. She didn't like to sew. She couldn't determine precisely what she was doing with her hands. It almost looked—but how ridiculous—as though she had nothing in her lap at all and that she was sitting completely vacant-minded cleaning the dirt from underneath her fingernails. The nail of her right index finger slowly scraped under that of her left thumb. No. She was sewing. That's what she should be doing. Even though she didn't enjoy it. She was sewing and listening to her husband read from the Bible. Outside the wind must be howling and the little ranch house was completely buried in snow. Here we are, she said to herself. Safe and warm and quiet. Oh, it's so quiet. Are we dead? I can't hear the wind at all except when it gusts and makes the stove whirr. My goodness, look at us. How long have we been here.

Against the rumbling noise of the washer outside, she strained to hear the quick suck of saliva in her husband's pipe, the creak of the loose rail on his rocker. Her child was drowsy from the intense heat from the stove. How long?

Bradley tottered over to her and stood quietly. When he bumped her leg, she flinched. That made her laugh. And she laughed again, a light burst of almost hysterical laughter. She made herself laugh again, higher still and more hysterical, to crack the vision.

'Here,' she said. 'Here I am.' She tapped the pump. Then, she said to Bradley, 'And I know what *you* want. You want some chocolate and a story. That's what.' She lifted him on to the counter so he could dangle his feet in the wash water.

'This is the story of the time Etilio decided to fight the most wicked Indian in the village,' she began.

While she spoke, Larkins came inside to get his water jug. For once, she was able to ignore him and continued telling Bradley the story. 'And then,' she said, moving away from the sink so Larkins could get his jug without touching her, 'Etilio cracked wicked Vitolan on the back with his magic stick and Vitolan was suddenly covered with feathers. All the village watched as Vitolan became huge and as his eyes became wild. His arms grew long and became wings and his legs shrunk and grew enormous sharp claws. Now he was even more dangerous than he was when he was only a man, because he snatched up a clawful of warriors and ate them as if they were worms. The more he ate, the bigger he got. Soon he was too big to sit in the trees. The branches cracked and broke. He sat on the walls of the village and they crumbled. So he moved into a cave in the mountains. Everyday he would swoop down on the village, darkening the sun, and fly away with his claws wiggling with warriors. "You made a mistake," the people of the village told Etilio. "You should not have turned Vitolan into a vulture." Seeing what he had done, Etilio said he was sorry for working a bad miracle and promised to get rid of Vitolan for ever.

'Now, Bradley, how do you think he did that?'

The little boy pointed across the room to his father's black powder rifle.

'Not that. There were no guns then. Only bows and arrows.'

'Arrows,' said Bradley.

'Not that. The arrows wouldn't go through Vitolan's feathers. Besides, he flew too fast and too high for arrows.'

Bradley kicked at a pot in the sink, splashing them both.

All the while, Larkins stood by the screen door holding his clay water jug. His flat, hard glare flickered now and again with signs of interest. Her story held him there against his will.

'It isn't right,' he said, at last.

She interrupted herself. 'What's that, Tommy. What isn't right?'

'You should be telling him something else. He shouldn't put his feet in the dish water.'

'Bible stories?' He doesn't like Bible stories all the time.'

Larkins was silent.

'Besides, I want to tell him this one.'

Larkins watched her eyes as he lifted the water jug above his head and let it drop onto the concrete.

At the dull sound of breaking crockery, Bradley let out his breath in a frightened wail. Louise embraced him. The tears which now fogged her vision made her husband seem large and curiously unstable. 'How dare you!' she screamed. But, he had let the screen close behind him. Through it, she watched him swagger back to work. He was whistling.

She found a sponge on the counter. Forcing the lump back down her throat, she continued. 'So one day, when nearly all of Etilio's people had been eaten by the giant vulture and the village was almost empty, Etilio went away to look for Vitolan.' Her voice broke and faltered. She was crawling on the floor, sopping up the mess. When thunder sounded outside and it began to pour rain, she didn't notice it.

'As he left, Etilio told his people, "There will be a sign. If you see a dust cloud big enough to hide the sun, Vitolan is gone forever. If the sky turns black and the sun leaks water, you will know I am dead and the Earth will freeze." So, Etilio travelled for many days before he found the vulture's cave, high in the Shinning Mountains. There, at the cave's entrance, he found a young woman. She must have been very pretty once, but now she was skinny and dirty and covered with bruises and cuts. With her was a small boy. Well, he was half boy and half bird.'

'Birdee,' said Bradley. 'Could he fly?'

'No. He wasn't old enough. The young girl,' Louise continued, 'was very glad to see Etilio. She told him she didn't like living in a cave in the mountains with a vulture. I wouldn't either. Just then Vitolan came flying home. He was so big that he covered the sun like a storm cloud. The young girl made Etilio hide. He turned himself into a cockroach and crawled into a crack in the cave's wall. After the young woman had fed the vulture, she called out to him to see if he was asleep. Vitolan. Vitolan. Vitolan? Are you sleeping?" When the vulture didn't answer, she whispered into the crack in the cave's wall telling Etilio that it was safe. Then, Etilio turned himself back into a man and killed the sleeping vulture by poking out his eyes with his magic stick and stinging his brain. Then he took the young woman and her little bird-boy outside the cave. He touched the little boy-bird and turned him into a boy. He touched the young woman and she became well and beautiful once again. Last of all, he cracked his magic stick against the entrance to the vulture's cave and the top of the mountain came down causing a huge dust cloud to rise into the blue sky darkening the sun so that the people in the village would know the vulture was dead. Then, Etilio took the young girl home with him and called her Bina, which means "Loved One." He called the little boy Tonia, which means "Little Witness". And they lived in the village for the rest of their lives.'

She was quiet then. By that time, the large dark thunderheads had passed over and the sun was beginning to knife through.

'Mummy's sad,' said Bradley.

'Only for a minute. Just a minute.' Impulsively, she did what she wanted to do when she watched him sleeping. She pulled him into her arms and held him tight, carressing his cheeks with her fingertips, rocking him, searching for comfort and strength. Rocking on the concrete floor of the mine office, she held him and wished that she could make the mine and the slag piles and the buildings suddenly disappear as easily as that. She wished she could make the mountain sink and that a dust cloud would rise and obscure the sun just long enough, Oh Lord, just long enough for her to get them down to the little ranch cabin. She would have a fire built in no time at all, and before the last haze of gray-blue dust was swept away by the wind, supper would be steaming on the rusty box stove.

V

Bradley broke free from her embrace and ran out the door.

Larkins looked up from the picking screen and saw his son followed by Louise running like mad toward him. He motioned for them to go away, as if he were batting away insects. She caught Bradley by his overall straps and swept him into her arms. 'Oh, no you don't. You're staying inside with me.' And she carried the wailing child back into the office. Even though it was hot inside and humid from the brief shower, she closed the door.

As she moved about the dim room a sensation of confinement, one which on previous days she had shrugged off as an inconvenience, began to build. He'd sent her inside. He'd flicked her away. He'd done that before. But, now it made her flush with anger and shame. She knew perfectly well it wasn't Elmer who wanted to work out of the sight and sound of women and children. Damn him.

By the time she had finished the lunch dishes and wiped the table and counter, her anger had focused itself enough for her to ask: Well, what is it? What do I prefer? Me. What do I need?

She tore the pasteboard backing off her note pad. Her handwriting was small but sharp.

'Tommy,' she wrote, 'What I want to say is this. It is about an attitude. I will be specific. You tell me that I cannot fertilize the garden. Feed the rabbits pellets. Buy Bradley sandals. All of this would cost about $15.00. You tell me this in a tone which insults me. You are abusive. Yet, is there ever any question of you buying your beer? Of playing cards with Elmer? Of buying that rifle with the washing machine money? Your hunting and card playing are your needs. I must respect them. But, I won't any longer if you don't stop bullying me about my needs. I am asking for no more than one-quarter of what you spend at cards and on beer in one month. I truly believe that the things I need will make our lives on this place better. I garden for pleasure. True. I know that I lose nothing and am almost certain we save something too. I cannot live here unless I know that I am building something which is at least semi-permanent. I want a home. A real home. I see now that I could make one on the ranch. I can do it here, too. But please, could you not play cards so often. Could you, perhaps, sacrifice a little? I won't ask you again. I mean . . . '

She slammed her palm onto the table. 'Damn it! Damn!'

Her son left his toy corner and wrapped his arms around her

legs nearly tilting her backwards in her chair. She restrained the urge to tear up the note and to hold him. 'Just a second, my darling. Mummy will be finished in just a second.'

'I mean I am not threatening you. I try and love you. I want to do what I enjoy, too.' She wrote rapidly, barely thinking. 'Try and respect that. That's all I ask. L.'

She rested the note against the pump handle where he would be almost certain to see it when he came in for water. She changed Bradley's diapers, found his backpack and their hats. Her stomach was nervous and excited—a sudden flight of butterflies. Bradley followed her down the path to the outhouse where she broke the rule. This time she left the door open and gazed down the valley where the ranch was. She had had her say. She had never dared to criticize him before. Well, now she had opened her mouth for good.

A feeling of boldness and rightness and strength filled her. She crossed the stream and approached the huge turquoise washer. The bright sunlight spirited her.

'I'm taking Bradley to town,' she yelled over the noise of the machine.

If Larkins heard her, he made no acknowledgement. However, Elmer, who was working elbow to elbow with her husband picking blue stone from the screen, interrupted himself long enough to wave no and tell her that he was quitting soon and needed the jeep himself.

'I'll go up the mine, then,' she said.

As she followed the stream up to the mine, she admired the small aspen trees. The odor of sage struck her once again. That particular smell had to be her favorite in all the world. It was so much more pleasing without the noise of the washer. She could hear the breeze and the rush of the small stream.

The mine shaft was brimming with grayish water. A blue vein of turquoise disappeared into the murk. The surface stone was virtually ruined because of its exposure to water and weather. But Louise knew that when they tunnelled they would find deep blue beautiful turquoise. She visioned veins as thick as her arm, veins spider-webbed with gold. She stood at the mine entrance and noticed that the thunderstorm had washed the dust away from the turquoise on the ground. The small stones scattered around her feet looked like blue tears. She took a small fruit jar out of her pocket and began to pick. Most of the stones were decomposed and crumbled like rotten cement in her fingers. Elmer could tell her if they were worth anything. With Bradley on her back, she scoured the shaft entrance over turning stones. At the head of the shaft, she forced a large flat rock onto its edge and sent it into the gray murk. She uprooted a small sage and shook out the roots. There had to be something of value there. There just had to be. She crawled on her hands and knees and began to dig for pieces.

And a half an hour later she did find something. Carrying Bradley in her arms so she could run faster, she took it to the men. She was out of breath and was radiant with excitement. Clutched in her fist was a large blue nugget. She handed the piece to Larkins, who handed it to Elmer. 'I found it on top of the shaft entrance. It was buried,' she said, still breathing hard. 'I must have looked there a hundred times, but I never dug before. It's a good one. It is. Isn't it, Elmer?'

Elmer smiled. He put the stone in his shirt pocket, buttoning the flap. 'It's a good one, Louise.' Then, he reached for his buckle and, still smiling, whipped off the belt. She heard it flap around his body. He unzipped the compartment and took out three five dollar bills. Larkins put his hand out. 'There you are, Boy. Give them to her.'

Larkins handed the money over to Louise, but didn't look at her face.

She wanted to believe he was proud of her and she waved the bills in his face like a fan to try and make him smile.

'Do you know what this means?' she said to neither of them. She squeezed Bradley and spoke into his hair. 'Now, we can get plastic to put over the window holes and rabbit pellets and a wash board. There may be enough left over for sandals for you. Elmer, are you sure it's not too much?'

'It's not too much.' He was replacing his belt. Larkins had resumed work. 'Not too much for Rio Cojos turquoise.'

She carried Bradley back to the mine office. The note she

had left by the pump was gone. Most likely, she thought, he read it and threw it in the trash. She looked in the steel garbage bucket. Well, he has it with him then. And so what if he showed it to Elmer. The thought did occur to her that the money was a bribe. Maybe the nugget wasn't worth anywhere near fifteen dollars. That didn't matter. The money was hers. Elmer had given it to her. Besides, she hadn't asked for it. Not really. Anyway, she needed it. It made things better–almost.

A short while later, she heard Elmer's jeep start and whine down the road toward Rio Cojos.

That was okay. She'd borrow the jeep tomorrow and go to town. She might go all the way to Salida or to Alamosa to shop.

As she prepared supper, the washer's noise wasn't so oppressive. She realized that she had skipped lunch entirely and opened a can of tuna fish. She ate quickly, direct from the tin with a small silver fork her mother had given her.

Soon, she began to cook supper for her husband who was now working under the lights at the picking screen. She would sweep the floor again. She would carry in more wood. She wouldn't stop until he stopped. Then, they would have supper. Supper in silence together with Bradley asleep in his sleeping box. Afterwards, no matter how she felt that night–rather, especially because she felt so elated–she knew that her husband would fall asleep in his chair with the leather covered Bible open in his lap not to be awakened by crying or by laughter or by the evening thundershower which she saw was building up in the mountains above the small, dim mine office where they were living.

VI

Day after day the endless revolving of the turquoise washer jarred and buffeted the stone, removing the clay from the gem. Outside the men, working under the shelter, picked through the slag depositing what blue stone they found into the pockets of white nail aprons tied around their waists. Toward the end of the summer, Elmer got sick and most days Larkins worked on the screen alone. He was fighting the season. There had already been one storm in the high peaks, and the snow was creeping down the mountains, leaving a morning dusting for the sun to melt. By then the shaft entrance was skimmed with ice. They had stayed up there too long already, but Larkins was pressing for more income. The assessment work was complete, and they had grossed upwards of two thousand in stone.

In early October, Louise asked to go back to the station, where it was warm, where Bradley had children to play with. Larkins stayed at the mine. She returned to her old job at the Lobo, and Bradley spent most of his waking hours with Mrs. Thurlow, whose bosom smelled like an ashtray. That fall she worked in a dream. They didn't seem to be going anywhere. She was a waitress again. It seemed they were going backwards.

One night, Louise was half asleep and heard her husband's low grumbling laughter echoing off the side of the building. He was supposed to be in bed up at the mine. Confused, she got up and turned on the light. Below her, parked at the pumps, she saw them through the windshield of the jeep. The woman sat behind the steering wheel, leaning against the door. Her husband's face was not visible, but Louise saw his green work shirt and knew that vulgar laugh, that low laughing grumble against flesh. Kitty had her arms open wide and her head thrown back, wedged between the seat and the door. Her mouth was open.

As much as she wanted to, Louise could not make herself move away from the open window. She did not wonder what he and Kitty were doing. She wanted to know why they were doing it there, why Larkins wanted to rub her face in it.

She stood at the window with the light at her back hoping that one of them would look up and see that she was watching. That's what he wanted. Wasn't it? She ached for her husband to discover her there. How she hoped it wouldn't be Kitty who saw her first. But, all Kitty had to do was to open her eyes and let her gaze drift up to the single light above her, and she would see a small white face and a body in too large pajamas no more than thirty feet away. Maybe the light was too strong behind her, and she would see nothing more than a silhouette and not the dumb surprise on her face which changed from disbelief to disgust as she watched and watched, listening to her husband's laughter diminish.

When Louise realized that Kitty was not going to open her eyes, Louise opened and closed the window as noisily as she could. She didn't look outside again to determine the effect. She cut the bedroom light. A few minutes later, she heard the jeep door slam. Next, she heard the door to the office open and the register ring. The desk drawer opened. A bottle or a glass smashed on the pavement below her window. And she lay, frightened now, praying that the door to their bedroom would not fly open. When it didn't, she put on a robe and went downstairs in the dark. She saw her husband stumbling to the jeep with bills in one hand and a bottle in the other. Only then did she realize that this is what he did when he came to town at night. Quite simply, he had forgotten or was too drunk to remember that she and Bradley were not at the mine anymore.

In the morning, she woke Bradley early and took him to Mrs. Thurlow's. She was waiting in front of the Lobo when the cook opened the doors. The memory of what she had witnessed the previous night had successfully dimmed itself until only a woman's open mouth, a steering wheel and the curve of her white neck along with the grumbling vulgar laughter exploding on flesh persisted. She was amazed how little emotion she felt. If anything, she found that she was relieved. She did care once, but that had stopped months ago. Seeing them together like that wasn't a revelation, it was an end–a blunt, deadening end.

In the next weeks, sometimes she consoled herself with memories of how he used to be before they moved to Rio Cojos or how he was during their early days there. How he would take a bath with a glass of whiskey on the window ledge. She thought it was funny then. She liked it when he left the door open. He took off all of his clothes except for his hat and poured a half a glass. His hands and face and neck were burned a deep red and the rest of his body was hard and white. He lowered himself carefully into the steaming tub and began to sing, his hat tilted back on his head. 'You take a bath the way you prepare a baked potato,' she remembered saying. 'The hell I do,' he said. 'This is a cowboy bath. It sucks the dirt right out of you. The whiskey lubricates.' 'You're as bad as Elmer Gill,' she said, loving him then, amazed by how easily he could adapt to the place. 'We live in Rio Cojos,' he said. 'When in Rome.' She was standing in the doorway wearing her waitress uniform. 'Most likely we'll always live here,' he told her, 'doing one kind of a job or another. You know, every time I see you dressed like that, like the only blonde Indian in the country, with your hair pulled into a net, you're good enough to eat, Babe. That hair of yours looks like a golden trout caught in a net. I love you, Babe. I surely do.' She'd walk into the bathroom then and let him pull her toward him, taking her neck in his warm wet hands. The taste of whiskey on his lips? For months, she told herself that all the men in Rio Cojos tasted like that. She had tried not to let it bother her. Besides, her husband never got in as bad a way as Elmer Gill did.

But, that couldn't go on forever. There is more to a person's life than waiting tables and reading the Bible and waiting for your husband to turn around and walk back into your life sober and clear eyed. He would be that way when he wanted to be. She couldn't do anything about it. For some time, Louise had realized she had made a mistake with her compulsive love for Larkins. Now, for the first time, she let herself consider the possibility. She didn't find that out for herself. It took a death to do that for her.

In early February of that year, her childhood nanny died. No one close to her had died before then, and the loss was enormous. She called her parents and asked to come back for Dorothy's funeral. No, Tommy didn't need to come, too. There was no question of Larkins going. 'Don't you see?' she said to them on the telephone in Thurlow's Drug Store, 'I'll have a chance to see you alone, to visit, just Bradley and me.'

The check for the ticket arrived. She wrote: 'I do wish I could bring us all. Our family is now one father, one mother (Me), one child, a cat, a jeep (adopted). At the moment your grandson is crying. He wants Tommy to come too, but even if he had known Dorothy, it's best that he stays here. There's no one to run the station. That's Bradley's reason for crying. He's not sick. Not that it can bother you. Strange idea that noise can be carried in a letter. I'm sorry to upset you. I can't concentrate. I'm too exhausted. For days and days, I felt that I've already left. Ha. Ha. I have quit my waitressing. When you see me, I'll be only me. Also, I cut off my hair. Bradley wears one of my pig tails pushed under his cap. It goes down his back like a snake.'

Louise surprised herself making the reservations.

'One way,' said the male's voice over the telephone.

'One way,' she said. 'Adult and child.'

She waited until it was time to go before she told Larkins what she had done. He took it the way she thought he would. He put on his coat. 'Fly carefully,' he said. 'I'll see you when I see you.'

Louise found it hard to determine if he was feeling anything at all. He didn't touch her. His embrace with Bradley was brief, almost cold, because the little boy pulled back from his father's kiss. She didn't need to ask him where he was going. He would go where he always went to spite her, to make her worry, to make her pay attention to him, to make her lonely and sad and ashamed of herself.

Though Louise and Bradley were both dressed for the trip, coats and mittens and hats, they had a few hours before they had to be at the airport in Alamosa. She had no idea whether or not Larkins would be back to drive her to the airplane or not. She supposed that he wouldn't. She had not said good-bye, not the way she wanted to. She hadn't put in her last word. When she thought about it, she couldn't very well call him at the Arsenal or at Kitty's.

'Dear Tommy, I'm saying good-bye now. I'll miss you. Stay well . . .'

No. She must tell him why. It was strange. She felt happy. She got up from the table and went into the bathroom and looked at herself in the medicine cabinet mirror. Raising the note, she tore it in half and let it drop into the sink. Before she had seen herself she had thought she looked like an old fashioned run-away, hat coat suitcase, a girl running away from home. But, the face she saw in the mirror surprised her. It wasn't drawn or teary or tired. Though she didn't feel the way she looked, she decided to act it. She had plenty of time. She gave Bradley a coloring book, which she intended to use for the flight, and gave Larkins what she thought was a true and sparky letter. It took her a few tries, but she had to get it right, whether he paid any attention to it or not. She had to have a last say.

'Dear Tommy—

'Do you know that trying to love you is like trying to wash your face with a small piece of soap? Not a motel size one, an airplane size one smaller than a fifty-cent piece. It takes concerted effort to get lather up from a bar that size. When you have it, you wonder what ever happened to the bar. Are you surprised? Did you ever expect I would leave you? You probably saw it coming a mile away. But, for so long I haven't cared. I have been sticking it out. My resistance was down for a while and I needed to get back my old strength. I just want you to know that I believe you left me first. You have been away from me for a long time.

'Now, why am I going? I'm going to tell you as precisely and as clearly as I can, even if you don't care.

'I have come to fear your actions. I can't predict you.

'Love, to me, is being dependent. Love, for you, does not go any further than you, yourself.

'I have some questions:

'How can I love someone I can't depend on?

'When you want "female companionship" you go to Kitty. I know that. When you want to talk, you play cards at the Arsenal. When you want to complain, you complain to me.

'Where are you at those times? Where are you when you are with Kitty? Where am I in your thoughts?

'I don't know how much you love her. But you love her enough to hurt me. She means too much, she is too important.

'So, I am staking no claim on you. None. I will not hold you I see that I can't hold you. I don't want to.

'My choice was a bad one. You are a punitive person. You want success or failure, only. You are obsessed. To live with you, I must be something I am not and do not want to become–compulsive and paranoid. I will not withdraw and obey you any longer. I will not become eccentric, submissive or weak. I will not lose my self-respect. Submitting to you has made me that way. In my heart, I know that I am not weak or obsessed.

'I admit it. I don't know how my life will end. But, I do know how I don't want it to end. You don't see the world as I see it. I don't think you want to anyway. This place is fine for you and your goals and I do not wish you bad luck. I don't wish you anything anymore. I don't want to know you. I am not fighting with you. I am too tired to quarrel. I feel disappointment in myself.

'There's no last word, no bitterness unless I make bitterness, which I don't want to do. I am relieved to be going and am thankful that I have the strength to go. My suffering and ignoring and servitude, however slight, which I gave you willingly as a trusting wife must have some meaning and it will only if I leave you behind. And I am leaving soon. I am not strong enough to stay with you any longer. I am not ashamed to say that. The safety of a home, however small or poor it is, is what I want. The rules you live by are too broad to allow for that and they are not my rules. I will never feel safe. I have never felt safe with you. We came out here to make a life, not a fortune. You can't have both. At least, not with me. I hope you will find someone who will tolerate you. I hope you will respect the strength it takes for me to leave.

'I am not sad. And I'm not especially happy or relieved, either. I'm afraid–I'll admit that–but not too afraid to see the world ahead of me, my life ahead of me. And, it's not such a bad future. I have Bradley to raise. I have a home I can go to for a while.

'I'll think of you, as you were in the past–as if you were dead and are a part of my past. Any more than that? Tears? Regrets? Yes, I expect so–yes. But, I am not wounded or bleeding or hurt. I have been hurt by you, but I am now healed and I have decided that I am strong enough to do what I am going to do. L.'

She folded the note and placed it in an envelope and set it by the sink. He would see it when he came back from Kitty's or the

Arsenal or where ever he was. As an after thought, she wrote on the outside of the envelope: 'I'm using the jeep. You can pick it up at the airport sometime. It seems better than calling a taxi.' That made her smile. How angry it would make him if she raided the cash register for a taxi ride to Alamosa.

In Denver, she changed planes from Frontier Airlines to United. She was surprised by how easy it was to leave Rio Cojos behind. Once the large aircraft was in flight, she could leave all of that and think of where she was going. Kitty, Elmer, the mine, the Shell station–Tommy, yes, even Tommy–dropped out of her mind with an ease which was almost as frightening as falling free from a great height must be. The ranch drifted into her thoughts, like a slowed tumbleweed. It might have saved them. Then, the ranch fell away behind her as well.

Dozing now, somewhere over Nebraska, she started when the stewardess served her lunch. Afterwards, Bradley received a pin and a play kit in a plastic bag. Louise admired her son. He was being such a good little man. Occupied and brave. But how fragile was his pose. It could break anytime and he could burst into tears. For now, though, he was busy coloring and didn't want to be fondled. She was glad she had him to worry about.

For the airplane flight, Louise wore jeans and a flannel shirt which belonged to her husband. Bradley had on his unpatched striped overalls which her mother had sent. In the sanitized atmosphere of the airplane's cabin, she realized that a faint odor of gasoline and oil hung about them both. Though she had washed everything twice in Mrs. Thurlow's washer and bathed twice in the tiny tub before boarding the plane, they still smelled like the Shell station.

She hoped that the thin, blonde haired man she was sitting next to was not offended. They smiled and spoke briefly during the flight. For the last few minutes, Bradley sat on the man's lap, interrupting his reading.

She knew she was larger, too. Her husband's shirt should not fit her as well as it did. She wished she had a dress and smelled like outdoors. Sage and clean, dry dust were much more pleasant smells to carry home. And she hoped, Oh Lord, that her own odor would be overlooked. They must give her time to wash her clothes again and to bathe with her mother's soaps before they judged her.

After all, the mine was behind her now. She had forced Rio Cojos and Tommy into her past. Still, moments of panic swept through her. She had become a fat dwarf. A petroleum soaked troll! So much had happened to her that maybe her mother and father would not know who she was.

Still, Louise knew, she would find herself hysterically cheerful when she got off the plane–any minute now–and ran, carrying Bradley and her backpack and shoulder bag, ran floppy in her jeans and flannel shirt, reeking to Heaven of grease and gasoline and probably a lot of other things, to bury herself in her parents' embrace.

As the dark low buildings of South Boston distracted her, she wondered if she would have been better off if she had remained home. She decided she wouldn't have been, not really. After all, she did have the strength, the will, to leave when she had to–she wasn't a victim, not really.

She repositioned Bradley who was asleep and was drooling on her leg.

And she knew that if her mother seemed worried about her or disappointed or noticed how much she had changed, she must ('Oh Lord, you must help me!') she would, take her mother's hands with strength and self-possession, and she would tell her mother that it was all right. So what if her life was different and unexpected, so what if she smelled differently because of the difference and the unexpectedness.

She felt the rumble of the wheel bays opening under her.

As they touched down at Logan, tears began to stream down her cheeks. She closed her eyes to squeeze them out 'Thank you,' she whispered. 'Oh Lord, thank you so much. I am so happy to be home.'

And quickly now, with Bradley under one arm and with what seemed to her like a hundred pounds of bags and sacks, she scrambled off the airplane leaving behind her the fat, gasoline-soaked troll, the flannel covered dumpling. All of that vanished when she saw her parents waving from the arrival area–waving blindly for they could not possibly see her through the brown tinged glass–vanished when she realized how enormously relieved she was to see them at last and to be home, home like a small girl again for a little while, home where she could rest and where there would not be troubles for a while at least.

Sisters

THEY LOOKED NO MORE like sisters than two women sitting next to one another on a bus. To hide a growing bald spot, Dorothy used to wear a lace scarf tied under her chin, secured at either temple with large silver bobby pins. The scarf was replaced first by a black hat and later by a bright green turban, but I'm getting ahead of myself.

Dotty lived with us and cooked our meals for as long as I can remember; Deedee usually visited on Sundays. Just as Dot was cleaning up from lunch, her sister would barge into the kitchen and collapse in the smallest chair with her dress hiked up on her knees and her brown stockings gathered at her ankles. They talked and laughed with such abandon that all the rooms in the house, a jumble of nooks and passageways, seemed to dislocate and reposition themselves around the kitchen. My father complained that their laughter penetrated the noise from his table saw. As I remember it now, Deedee always carried with her an animal, which was lost in the pendulous folds of her arms. Over the years, there were two cats, a small spaniel, a bulldog named Pug, and a parrot, and so on, all of which she over-fed, petted to distraction, smothering them as it were in her two-hundred-odd pounds of folds and white fat. I have always thought that Deedee is the sort of person who uses up her pets the same way some women consume lovers–intense passion followed by a blinding flare-out, which leaves no trace of the old. Any number of lost, weakened, vagrant dogs, cats, birds, rodents have found her and lived out the last of their days smothered by her attention. It is attention. I can't call it love. Deedee is too smothering.

Some Sundays Albert McGrath, Deedee's long-time boy–friend, would drive her down from Epping, others she'd take the bus. Always, my father left out the wine from lunch for them. If he forgot, Deedee could easily cajole her sister into raiding the liquor closet.

I don't know how many Sunday afternoons I watched from my bedroom window as Deedee struggled up the hill from the bus stop. Slowly waddling under her enormous weight, she carried a brown sack for her shoes and a half pint of peppermint schnapps, which dangled in her small hand like a mitten. I'd rush down to the kitchen where Dot was blushing with excitement. As Deedee climbed the porch steps, Dot straightened her white scarf, smoothed her apron, and began to fumble with something in the sink. Then, Deedee threw open the door, piled her coat in the pantry, and pulled the smallest chair into the center of the kitchen and collapsed. She was breathing heavily from the exertion of the walk and was unable to change into her shoes until she had rested.

'I swear to Christ,' she said. 'I wish one of us knew how to drive. That hill will get my ass one day.'

'You shouldn't talk like that,' said Dot, pretending to be busy, waiting for her happiness to diminish. She so anticipated her sister's visits that she was embarrassed to show how much, but Deedee wasn't fooled for a minute. Her eye for her sister's devotion was as keen as it is for lost animals.

Once Deedee had recovered her power of speech, she changed into her shoes and threw a boot at Dot's rump. 'Come on, you old drudge. Don't work so hard. The place is spotless as it is. Where's the wine? I'm damn dry from the ride. Where's your manners?'

We didn't live extravagantly in those days, but my father enjoyed wine for Sunday lunch, and it wasn't without deep pride and an awkward attempt at sophistication (that same matinee manner she feigned when she wore her green turban) that Dot replied, 'I served the family an acceptable California white at lunch. Dry and slightly nutty. There seems to be just a half a litre on ice.'

I took for granted the way we lived then–comfortable but modest. Still, I had an idea of Deedee's way of life and knew that for her to sit in our kitchen was a step up for her.

'Why, you sly bitch,' said Deedee. 'You held it back on them. Robbing these rich folks of their precious wine. Hell, let's knock off that bottle and get into my schnapps. What a week I've had. Good Jesus, what a week. You'll die laughing.'

Dot was to use only the kitchen dishes and the stainless. But, on Sundays she lapsed and brought out the cut glass from the pantry, knowing how much more grand her sister felt sitting in the breakfast room sipping wine and then schnapps from

Waterford glass instead of fruit jars.

Gradually, it seemed Dotty spent less time in the kitchen. While once she would fuss about after supper, hoping one of us would join her to talk, towards the end she went directly to her room after she got the dishwasher running. She stopped wearing the small white cloth fixed with bobby pins to cover her bald spot. Only when Mother mentioned it to her did she begin to wear that ridiculous black hat the size of a child's Easter basket. By that time, she was spending all of her free time in her room.

One evening, I was alone in the den and could hear Dot's television above me. Over the muffled noise from the set, I heard a thumping. It sounded like shoes were being scattered over the floor. The noise went on for some time. When it stopped, I heard Dot scream. Not a scream of fear, but a child-like cry.

I whispered at the door 'Dotty, are you all right?' and knocked before I let myself in. The large television screen illuminated the entire wall with colored light, diminishing the cosmetics on her small vanity, throwing an unnatural light on the photographs Dot had framed of my family and the porcelain figurines she collected. The light was on in the bedroom. I went in there first. An acid, rotten fruit smell came from the tub. I tried to rinse it away, but the hot water only made it worse. Then, the hangers in the closet clanged. I had to move aside a pile of shoes to get to the door. From the darkness within, my Dot peered up at me from between the hems of her uniforms. She was smiling, blissfully drunk. 'Dotty overdid it,' she said.

I helped her up, cleaned her face, and lifted her onto the bed, tucking a blanket around her so she wouldn't roll onto the floor.

'Poor Dorothy,' she said. 'Nobody loves old Dorothy.'

'Hey, silly. I do.'

But, she was asleep.

The following morning she was unusually quiet and cooperative. She wore her black hat and a fresh uniform. Without explaining myself, I helped her prepare breakfast and, by so doing, I suppose that I became her accomplice. At least I felt like one, because from that time on, when my parents went out for the evening, Dotty drank herself stupid in front of her television and I helped her off the floor of her closet to bed.

'Don't ever tell on me,' she whispered. 'You must never tell on poor unhappy Dot.'

And I've kept my word and have not spoken of her troubles until now. She was so fragile yesterday. Rather her body looked so very thin and fragile. She looked like a sleeping puppy. Safe, relaxed, but how terribly fragile, lying in that musty parlor room in Epping.

Though I have never told my parents about Dotty's binges, they must have found her in the closet themselves. Mother began to hint that what with my getting older and all, there might not be good reason for her to stay on with us.

Dorothy was incapable of comprehending her own retirement, so Mother threw herself to the task. She bought Dot new luggage. She took her shopping for dishes, pots, utensils. She reserved some of Dot's wage to be doubly certain she had a supplement to her social security. When it came time for Dotty to leave us, she seemed perfectly convinced that her retirement had been her idea alone.

We gave her a retirement supper, and she took my father's place at the head of the table.

'We're certainly going to miss you around here,' Mother said. 'I can't believe you are actually leaving. How will we ever make do without your help?'

Dot had had rum at cocktails and two glasses of wine with supper, followed by brandy with the cheesecake. At first, the drink did not phase her. She accepted more brandy from Father, who seemed slightly embarrassed for her.

'Now, you take care, old girl,' Father said, refilling her glass, joking with her, trying to smile. 'You take care, and I'll do the same.' He said this with no trace of warning or malice in his voice.

Dorothy took a long swallow and pushed the glass towards the centrepiece. She leaned back in her chair. Her unusually docile, large moist eyes now held a glimmer of defiance. 'Dot's a regular case,' she said, slurring slightly. 'Isn't she, now? You think your Dot's going to pot. That's what you're thinking. I know you are. All of you. Well, I can polish off this brandy and two more like it and balance this God damn glass on my head all the way down to Manchester and back again like a lady.' She laughed at that, proud and thoroughly relaxed. 'But, I better be good tonight,' she said in a childish voice. 'I don't want to sleep in the closet. No closet for Dotty tonight.' She was swaying in her chair by this time. Without the arms for support, she might easily have fallen onto the floor.

Father signalled for me to clear the table.

But, how could he know the times I had found her just like that, just as cheerful and jolly, just as drunk, beaming up at me from the floor of her closet between the hems of her uniforms. How could he know that as a child Dot had been sent to her closet as punishment, that as a girl she had been forced to spend entire days in her closet and that it was Deedee who secretly visited her and closed herself inside with her and comforted her and brought her nourishment.

Mother poured the coffee. I didn't want to listen when Dot told us, 'Where am I going? Why, of course, I'm going to live with my sister. Who else?' Deedee lives in two barren rooms in an old building in Epping, New Hampshire, an hour and a half away. 'But, I won't have anything to do,' she said. 'Sure, I'll cook for us, but she doesn't eat. There's no cleaning, not really. The place is too small to get dirty. That's why I'm glad you people will have me down to help out sometimes. Now, that's work.' She was rocking from side to side in her chair now, as if she were in a trance. 'We used to have some real times. Didn't we, Missus? Why, I'd have a roast all ready and cooking slow and you'd up and turn the oven on high and without fail, when you all reeled into supper at nine o'clock, like I knew you would, all lit up like candles, the meat would be gray. Gray right through. Ah, what does it matter any more. You always complained. Even if I cooked it perfect, you complained. Those were happy times for me. I'll tell you that. I never knew what was going to happen around here next. I call that work.'

Life in Epping changed Dotty. Living with that sister of hers accelerated her aging. No matter how hard Dot tried, she could not arrest the stagnant smell of disuse, the decay in the building which crept into the clothes. All the dusting she did, the waxing and cleaning for herself and her sister was a weak barrier. The odor of her rooms engulfed her. And Dotty brought that particular odor with her to our house the few times Mother asked her down to cook for a party. Though the family never spoke of it, the particular odor Dot brought down with her from Epping used to hang for days in our kitchen. I knew it couldn't be helped and didn't mind it, not really. I dismissed it by saying that after all Dotty must have smelled the way we smell when she lived with us and, naturally, she smelled different because she had gone away. The reason Mother finally stopped asking Dorothy down to help out with the supper parties was not for the reason she gave me. Quite simply Dot had not grown too slow; she had not become clumsy and absent minded–she always was that. She was forever forgetting to heat the soup; she always dropped spoons on the table when she was serving; she was notorious among Mother's friends for losing casseroles. The real reason Mother let her go for good was because Mother found it unspeakable that Dorothy was living in that obscene building in a town with open sewers with a sister who did nothing but drink and go to the race track. That's what made Mother stop asking Dot down to help. It didn't have anything to do with Dot. It was Epping and the odor of disuse that cancelled, in Mother's view, any of Dot's remaining charm–a charm which surfaced only momentarily toward the end as a shadow in her large dark eyes and in her voice.

I can't help but ask, would Dorothy have been any better off if she had stayed home with us? I don't think so, not really. She was bound to end up the way she did. Living with us, I suppose, may have arrested her change, little more than that.

The last time I spoke with her, her hair had fallen out and her face was swollen, along with her ankles. She had become if not identical to her younger sister, then, at least, as round and as unsure-footed. She had replaced the small Easter basket hat with a shiny green turban which she held closed in front with a bright glass pin. Her eyes were the only part of her which never

changed. Large and liquid, they almost allowed me to ignore
the other changes-the matinee matron's turban, the swelling,
the odor.

'You look worried,' she said that last time. 'Louise, you don't
have to worry. I have a fine life here. In fact, it's a hell of a lot
better than I thought it would be.'

She knew I didn't want to go up to their rooms, so we talked
in the parking lot.

I asked Dotty where her sister was.

'Christ, she's never here. You know Deedee and her God
damn horses.' Then, Dot began to laugh. 'Well, well,' she said,
after a moment. 'Aren't I a sight. I even talk like her.'

The green turban was weaving like a drunkard on her head,
but she laughed like she always did, as raucous and as loud as
she used to on Sundays at home with her sister, tears streaming
down her cheeks.

Yesterday, I drove up to Epping for the funeral. And I must
say that I have never seen her look more relaxed, so like herself,
so awfully peaceful. Lying there in the musty parlor, she looked
asleep like some quiet puppy Deedee might have found
wandering the streets, lost and hungry.